W9-BLS-746

Crime in a
COLORADO Cave

Books in the X-Country Adventure series

X-COUNTRY ADVENTURES

Crime in a COLORADO Cave

Bob Schaller

Baker Books

A Division of Baker Book House Co
Grand Rapids, Michigan 49516

© 2000 by Bob Schaller

Published by Baker Books
a division of Baker Book House Company
P.O. Box 6287, Grand Rapids, MI 49516-6287

Printed in the United States of America

All rights reserved. No part of this publication may be reproduced, stored in a retrieval system, or transmitted in any form or by any means—for example, electronic, photocopy, recording—without the prior written permission of the publisher. The only exception is brief quotations in printed reviews.

ISBN 0-8010-4453-7

Library of Congress Cataloging-in-Publication Data is on file at the Library of Congress, Washington, D.C.

For current information about all releases from Baker Book House, visit our web site:

http://www.bakerbooks.com

Contents

"Hot" Crystals from a Cold Cave

Ashley Arlington tucked a strand of blond hair behind one ear, ducked her head beneath the rocky outcropping, and lifted her lantern to better illuminate the chamber she had just entered. Stalactites hung from the ceiling like strange icicles, and stalagmites rose from the floor to meet them. The wind howled as it blew through the cave, and shadows dissolved and re-formed in the light of the flickering lantern.

Suddenly Ashley felt a firm tug on her shirtsleeve. Startled in the dark, moist cave, she turned in fright.

"Watch out—the bats are attacking!" said her brother, Adam, in a loud whisper.

Seventeen-year-old Ashley slugged her brother in the shoulder. The lean, five-foot-ten Ashley was one of the top athletes at Thomas Jefferson High School near the family home in Washington, D.C. She was aggressive on both the basketball and volleyball courts; however, those games weren't played in dark caves.

"You didn't scare me," Ashley said defensively. "But you have to admit, Adam, as beautiful as these caves are, they do kind of give you the creeps."

Sixteen-year-old Adam nodded his head and shivered. He wished he had worn jeans instead of shorts. But he had forgotten that the temperature inside the cave would be fifty-four degrees—as it always is—even on a June day when the temperature outside hovered around ninety degrees.

By this time the tour guide had moved out of the chamber and was heading back toward the entrance to Cave of the Winds in Manitou Springs, Colorado. Ashley and Adam followed with the rest of the tour group. Ever since the kids could walk, their family had taken at least two vacations each year. In the past, all the activities had been done with their parents, Alex and Anne Arlington. This summer the Arlingtons had driven their motor home to a campground in central Colorado and had pulled their sport utility vehicle behind it. From the campground they set out in their SUV to see as much of the state as they could.

For the first time, Mr. and Mrs. Arlington were giving Adam and Ashley some independence, letting them take the SUV on their own at times. Mr. and Mrs. Arlington spent those days with old friends who now lived in Colorado Springs. They visited museums and libraries, as well as frequenting coffee shops around town. The family still spent a few days together each week sightseeing. With this new sense of freedom, Adam and Ashley were excited to be in Colorado—and at Cave of the Winds.

Whoosh! Another cool gust blew a shiver up Adam's spine, and his teeth began to chatter.

"Hang on, Adam, we're almost there." Ashley grinned as the tour moved out of the unlit passageways and into the lighted areas of the main cave. As they walked toward the cave entrance, Ashley noticed that the man in front of her was wearing a sweatshirt that read "CU Women's Basketball Assistant Coach." Ashley was entering her senior year in high school and was hoping to play college basketball. Just as she was about to tap the man on the shoulder, one of the staff members working at the admission counter came running over, waving his hands.

"Wait, please! Ladies and gentlemen, please, stay where you are!"

Ashley shot Adam a confused look. "What do you think is going on?" she asked.

"I couldn't tell you," Adam replied. "And even if I could, I'd rather tell you when we were *outside* in the sun!"

Ashley smiled but wasn't sure what to make of the excited man in the Cave of the Winds staff shirt. Sirens wailed in the distance, growing louder by the second, and it started to appear that the situation really was serious. Soon two cars bearing the El Paso county sheriff's logo sped up the winding road toward the cave. The sirens' noise was amplified as it ricocheted off the face of the mountain, and Ashley was tempted to cover her ears.

Two officers got out of their cars and walked quickly toward the cave entrance as the staff member ran over to meet them.

"They're gone!" he said frantically. "Both of them, gone!"

Ashley thought that a couple had disappeared while spelunking deep inside the cave.

"I hope they find them," she whispered to Adam. "I wonder if they're from around here or if they're tourists like us."

Adam looked at the sheriff's deputies. A stocky blond man was talking quietly to the staff member, trying to calm him down. A tall, slender Hispanic man was listening intently.

"I don't know, Ashley," Adam said. "If someone is lost, why isn't anyone looking for them yet? And what if they're children? That would be so awful. Let's see if there's anything we can do to help with the search."

The staff member was now calmer and was walking with the blond deputy. The cave visitors had formed small groups and were talking among themselves, looking frequently at the deputies. Another worker, a middle-aged man with graying hair on the sides of his balding head, had emerged from the gift shop. He nodded yes to a question from the Hispanic deputy, then shook his head no. The man seemed nervous and barely spoke to the deputy, if at all. As the Hispanic deputy headed for the blond deputy and the first staff member, Ashley and Adam stepped toward him.

"Excuse me, sir," Ashley began. "We're both in good shape, and we could help look for whoever is missing."

"That's nice of you to offer, but it's not necessary," said the deputy, whose nameplate on his shirt read "Martinez."

"If no one is lost," Adam said, "then what's all the fuss about?"

"Please wait here for a few minutes," the deputy replied, and he walked over to join the other two men.

"Ashley," Adam said, "do you think he could be Paul Martinez, Dad's friend from Army Reserve days? Dad said he works as a Colorado law enforcement officer. Remember Dad was going to look him up while we're here so they could catch up on old times?"

"That's right!" said Ashley excitedly. "Let's see if we can find out Deputy Martinez's first name and ask him about Dad. Maybe if he is Dad's old friend he'll tell us more about what's going on."

From where they were standing, Ashley and Adam could hear the three men talking. The staff member, who had the name "Jim" embroidered on his shirt, turned and pointed to an enclave about thirty feet from the cave entrance.

"They were in there," he explained to the deputies. "We've been constructing the exhibit for a few weeks, but today was the first day the gold specimens were actually in place."

Gold? Adam and Ashley stared at each other in surprise. Adam had noticed two pieces of rock in the enclave, mostly because of their difference in coloration. Although the rocks were set fairly far back in the enclave, a glimmer in them had caught his eye. He never imagined that the glimmer might be something valuable.

"They're called gold crystals," Jim was explaining to the deputies. "The gold is mingled with mineral crystals. We found them when we were installing some safety features in a remote chamber that's currently off-limits to the public. Although they found gold crystals in Cripple Creek during the gold rush days, we never thought we'd find any here. The value depends on the quality of the specimen and the type of crystals in it; the insurance appraiser said ours were probably worth about $3,000 an ounce."

Ashley and Adam could see Deputy Martinez's eyebrows shoot up. "And how large were your two pieces?" he asked.

Jim turned and looked to see if anyone was watching or listening. Ashley and Adam quickly looked away. The other visitors were out of earshot. No one but Ashley, Adam, and the deputies could possibly hear Jim's reply.

"The smaller one and the larger one together are valued at half a million," he said so quietly that Ashley and Adam had to strain to hear him.

The two stared at each other as Adam quickly did the math in his head.

"Ash, those are a couple of big rocks to carry off and hide," he whispered. "There's no way a thief could fit them in his pocket!"

"Do you know how the thieves got past your security?" Martinez asked.

Jim looked down at the cave floor. "We were still putting the finishing touches on the exhibit," he said. "A man came up to the workers who were installing the security system and asked if they had seen his little boy. They said they only turned away for a moment to answer him, but when they turned back, the gold crystals were gone. The man who distracted them had also disappeared."

By now other officers had begun to arrive and interview the tourists. Adam and Ashley gave their names and home address to a female deputy, then explained that they were vacationing in Colorado with their parents. She took down the name of the campground where the Arlingtons' motor home was parked and also asked for their cell phone numbers. As the deputy searched their backpacks, Adam told her that he had noticed the "rocks," but neither he nor Ashley could give her any information about the theft. The deputies were carefully questioning and searching all the other tourists who had been present at the time of the theft as well. After a long wait inside the cave, Adam and Ashley were finally told that they could go outside.

They made their way toward the parking lot, and other visitors slowly began to trickle out of the cave after them. Adam and Ashley watched as people slowly headed for their vehicles. They could just see the area at the bottom of the hill where another sheriff's car was blocking the entrance road to Cave of the Winds, with a state highway patrol sedan not allowing anyone else up the hill.

Although Adam was finally warmed by the late afternoon sun, he was chilled by the thought of what had happened.

"Ashley," he said, "how could someone do something like this?"

"I don't know what they were thinking," she replied, "but I do know that what they did was wrong."

Two police officers searched the Arlingtons' vehicle. Then they were cleared to leave.

"I wish there was something we could do," Adam said.

"Let's just hang out for a minute," Ashley suggested. "We haven't had a chance to talk to Deputy Martinez about Dad yet, and you know, Adam, maybe there is something we can do."

As the people piled into their cars, Ashley pulled a journal and two pens from her backpack. Adam quickly caught on to her idea, dug into his own backpack, and pulled out a notebook.

"Here," Ashley said, handing her brother a pen. "Make notes of all the cars' license plates. Try to get a look at who is getting into each car, what they're wearing, how old they are—just anything and everything you see."

That would be easy. Although the cave was usually packed, especially during the summertime, it wasn't too crowded on this day. A big parade, a rodeo, and a convention were being held in Colorado Springs, which thinned the crowd at Cave of the Winds.

Adam and Ashley walked over to where Jim and Deputy Martinez were still talking. As the cave's staff began to leave, Jim gave Deputy Martinez their names. The middle-aged man with gray temples got into a compact car. The license plate on the back wasn't visible on the dirty vehicle, which was red with clay and covered with a thick coat of plain dirt as well. The car's owner, Jim told the deputy, was Kevin Yarbrough. A beautiful Asian woman, Kim Young, climbed into a red sport utility vehicle. Tom Ramsay and Rich Anderson both climbed into an ancient sports car. A girl from the gift shop got into a small pickup truck. That girl's name, Jim said, was Kelly Yeardly.

People were getting frustrated as the police thoroughly searched their belongings and their cars. The police didn't have time to run a radio check on every car, but they did get a license number from each vehicle to run as soon as the dispatcher had a chance.

"How much longer is this going to take?" an impatient older woman asked a policeman. "At least tell us what you're looking for," she said.

"I can't do that, ma'am," the patrolman said, closing the trunk of her Cadillac. "Thanks for your patience."

The woman and her husband grumbled as they got into the car and drove away.

Texas license plate, Adam wrote. *Older man, older woman (irate), two total in cream-colored Cadillac.*

The cars and trucks left one by one. Adam and Ashley wrote down all the details. "One car from New Mexico—'the Land of Enchantment'," Adam said, reading the license plates under his breath. "One from South Dakota—'Great Faces, Great Places' on that plate. One from New York with the Statue of Liberty on it. Three from Colorado with the county on each plate, and, of course, there's us, from the District of Columbia."

"Do you really have to write our own information down?" Ashley asked Adam. He smiled sheepishly.

"You did say everyone," he answered.

One man that Ashley distinctly remembered seeing on the cave tour hadn't yet passed the roadblock to leave, and she didn't see him among those remaining.

"Excuse me, sir," Ashley said as she approached the man in the University of Colorado basketball shirt. "Do you remember the man in front of you on the tour? He was short and stocky."

The man turned and looked at Ashley.

"Remember him?" the man asked. "Oh yeah, I remember him—he was wearing a denim jacket with the sleeves cut off. He talked to that couple."

The man in the basketball shirt pointed in the direction of an African-American and his Asian wife, who also said they remembered the short, stocky man quite well.

"My wife tried to make small talk with him, and he wouldn't even acknowledge her," he said. "He was awfully rude."

Ashley called Deputy Martinez over to join her group. He introduced himself as Deputy Paul Martinez to the man, Tom Bellarmine, and his wife, Jo Bellarmine. Tom relayed the story to Martinez.

"Did the man say anything to you, anything at all?" Martinez asked.

"No," Jo said, glancing at her husband for confirmation that he, likewise, had heard nothing. Martinez thanked the Bellarmines and then cleared them to leave.

"Wait a minute," Jo said as she reached for the door to their sport utility vehicle, which sported Colorado plates. "He did ask the tour guide just after the start of the tour if there was a rest room close by. She told him it was back at the gift shop. He left, I thought just to go to the bathroom. But we never saw him again."

Adam and Ashley looked at each other—a clue had been found.

"You know, he had a pretty thick accent," Jo continued.

"Did it sound like he was from a foreign country?" Martinez asked.

"No," Jo said as she shook her head. "It sounded like he was from New York, totally an East Coast accent. I have a sister in New York, and when I visit her, I hear that accent everywhere we go."

Adam looked at his list of plates.

"Two from New York!" he exclaimed. "One from New Jersey."

"We appreciate your help," Martinez said to the Bellarmines. "We'll be in touch if we need anything else."

The Bellarmines headed down the road. The officers seemed to be wrapping up their investigation of the tourists and their cars, so Ashley and Adam took the time to ask Deputy Martinez if he knew their father.

"My dad was in the Army Reserves with a man named Paul Martinez," Adam said to him. "Was that you, Deputy Martinez? Do you remember Alex Arlington?"

"Of course!" Deputy Martinez said. "We were good friends back then." After learning the Arlingtons were vacationing in the area, he said, "I can't wait to talk to your father! But would you have him call me at home later? I need to get back to work right now." He scribbled his office and home phone numbers on Ashley's notepad and hurried off with a smile and a wave.

Ashley and Adam hopped in their vehicle. Although a policeman had waved them out and down the hill, they sat for a minute and stared straight ahead. Adam was looking south through a pair of binoculars they kept in the car, and Ashley started to thumb through her notes. The sun had dipped far enough in the west to cast shadows where

Adam and Ashley were perched on the east side of the hill. Suddenly Adam leaned forward.

"Hey, do you see any roads over there on the hill?" he asked, his eyes still pressed against the binoculars.

Ashley looked up and shook her head no.

"Then what, could you tell me, is that vehicle doing over there?" Adam asked as he pointed out the front window.

Ashley could see only a small cloud of dust in the distance down by Highway 24. The highway was less than a quarter mile from the entrance to the winding road that led up to Cave of the Winds. She grabbed the binoculars from Adam.

"Did you see the license plate?" she excitedly asked Adam.

"I couldn't," Adam said. "All you can see is a cloud of dust behind the car."

Ashley pressed her eyes against the binoculars. At first, she thought the car was just four-wheeling. But it was heading down the hill very quickly, and the driver was obviously not familiar with the area. The vehicle bounced about, getting tossed around the dirt road and coming close to spinning out several times.

"Adam, go tell Deputy Martinez about this," she said. Adam got out of the SUV and ran toward Martinez, who was across the parking lot near the cave entrance.

"Deputy Martinez!" Adam hollered loudly. "DEPUTY MARTINEZ!"

Martinez was on his radio, which was attached near the epaulet on his uniform shirt. Adam told him about the vehicle they had seen traveling down the hill.

"Let's go!" Martinez said to Adam.

They started running, but Adam slipped. He had a white residue from the limestone in the cave on the bottom of his sneakers and had to rub them on the ground before trying to catch up with Martinez.

"Did you see the car or get a license plate?" Martinez gasped as he ran up to the driver's side of the SUV.

"Just going out of sight now," Ashley said.

Martinez radioed down to the deputy at the bottom roadblock, who immediately pulled out and gave chase with his lights flashing and siren screaming.

Martinez looked through the binoculars, but the vehicle was too far away and traveling much too fast for him to get a good look any longer. He asked Ashley what she had seen.

"I saw that it was a black sport utility vehicle, but it wasn't like this one," Ashley said. "I think it was a Toyota 4Runner. And the license plate was white with some blue lettering and a little red on it."

"No number?" Martinez said.

"Hey, I was lucky to see that much," Ashley said as Martinez returned the binoculars to her through the window. "The vehicle was kicking up a big cloud of dust from the dirt road. The driver spun out and stopped just after Adam went to get you. That created an even bigger cloud of dust. But before he pulled away, the dust went down for a second, and that's when I saw the color of the vehicle and the license plate's color. Oh yeah, the car also had a couple of antennas on it."

"A couple of antennas?" Martinez asked.

"Yes, one was smaller, like for a car phone," Ashley said, "and I think the other one was for a CB or shortwave radio or something like that."

As the trio talked, the call came back over the deputy's radio that the vehicle had been spotted coming off the hill. The officer chasing the car had spun out trying to make up ground on the vehicle by cutting a corner before entering Interstate 25 southbound. By the time the closest state trooper joined the chase, heading north on I-25 perhaps twelve miles south of where the black SUV was supposed to be at that time, the suspect's vehicle had already exited the interstate.

But to where?

"It's possible that the black 4Runner was somehow involved," Martinez said. "The deputy chasing it confirmed a New York license plate with two men inside. The passenger may have been the man you described."

"Oh yeah," Adam said, catching the deputy's attention.

"What is it?" Martinez asked Adam.

Adam turned toward Ashley. She saw in his deep brown eyes that he had remembered something.

"I did see that guy when he was leaving," Adam said. "I thought it was such a waste of money to leave when the tour was just getting started. I should've thought that something . . ."

"Now wait," interrupted Martinez. "There's no way you could've known that."

The radio chirped. A helicopter had been brought in to aid in the search for the mysterious vehicle. However, the black 4Runner was nowhere to be found. It could have made Pueblo in less than an hour, disappearing in rush hour traffic on I-25, or it could have taken a handful of exits in Pueblo.

The Colorado Springs police department, the state highway patrol, and the Pueblo police were alerted to be on the lookout for a black, late model Toyota 4Runner with New York plates.

That wasn't much to go on, and the police knew it. Deputy Martinez said good-bye to Ashley and Adam, thanking them for their help and reminding them to have their dad call him later. He then headed back toward the cave. He still had several hours of work ahead of him, investigating the crime scene and reviewing the information from the interviews.

As the dashboard clock registered 7:00 P.M., Adam and Ashley headed down the hill, late to dinner with their parents. They had little in their stomachs but a lot on their minds.

Going for the Gold

"You guys are late. What happened?" Anne Arlington asked as her two children got out of the car. The family's campground was just north of the Air Force Academy, a stone's throw outside the Colorado Springs city limit.

"Who wants chicken, and who wants steak?" Alex Arlington asked as he emerged from behind the motor home, using the camper as a wind break. As daylight continued to fade, the afternoon warmth turned to the gentle cold of evening.

Ashley and Adam placed their orders, then sat down near their mother as their father turned back toward the grill.

"We spent some extra time at Cave of the Winds today," Ashley began.

"Oh, that place is so beautiful," Mrs. Arlington said as she sliced tomatoes for a salad. "Your father and I went there years ago. Actually, you kids went, too. I think you were six, Ashley, and your brother was five. I've read a lot about the history of that place."

"Well," Adam said flatly, "you'll be reading even more about it in the paper tomorrow."

"What? Why is that?" their father asked.

"Dad, it was so exciting," Adam said. "There were these crystal rocks in an enclave—that's like a hole in the wall."

"Adam," his father said, "I know what an enclave is."

"Anyway," Ashley continued, her blue eyes squinting intently, "these crystals were mixed with gold—they were worth almost half a million dollars—and somebody stole them."

"Gold?" her father, an attorney, asked. "Let me get this straight. Someone is carrying around a half million dollars in gold crystals taken out of a cave halfway up a small mountain?"

Ashley and Adam nodded in agreement.

"We helped the police, and we met someone you know," Adam said proudly. He described what had happened after the theft and told their parents about meeting Paul Martinez.

"Whoa, wait a minute," their father said. "It's terrific that you ran into Paul Martinez—I was going to look him up anyway, and now you've got his number for me. But you aren't law enforcement agents. You don't have that power or that protection. I suggest this little adventure with these 'hot' rocks ends before it starts."

Ashley looked the other way, her feelings a bit hurt.

"Dad, I would hardly call half a million in gold a 'little adventure,'" she said, "and Deputy Martinez really appreciated our help!"

"Ashley," her father said quietly, "we're proud that you helped and that you want to do the right thing. But we also want you to be safe. Paul Martinez and the police can take it from here. Maybe he'll be able to give us an update on the criminal investigation when I call him."

"Why don't you two go inside and warm up a bit before dinner?" Mrs. Arlington suggested. "We're going to the Royal Gorge tomorrow and then to Cripple Creek."

On any other day that would have sounded quite inviting to Adam and Ashley. The Royal Gorge is the world's highest suspension bridge at 1,053 feet. The family could take the rail system to the bottom of the gorge after walking across the wooden bridge itself. And Cripple Creek had changed from a burned-out ghost town to a booming tourist attraction since the family had visited there during Adam's and Ashley's childhood.

Inside the camper, Adam logged on to the Internet on his computer. His grey laptop was equipped with a battery pack and a wireless modem; Adam took it almost everywhere with him. He looked up Cave of the Winds and then checked the computer atlas of the area surrounding Colorado Springs.

Ashley soon walked to the back of the motor home to see what Adam was doing.

"What are you looking for?" she asked.

Adam traced the possible routes out of Colorado Springs for the 4Runner. He hated to think that he and his sister could have helped solve the crime but had been pulled from the chase before it had really started. Actually, the information the police had was so sketchy, the chase might actually be over before it began anyway.

The pair monitored the evening news that night. Every local station ran a story on the theft, but none of them provided any new information. Tired, the family retreated to bed, thinking that the next day wouldn't be as exciting as this one had been.

Rather than cook in the motor home like they usually did, the family got up, went for a morning run, and then ate biscuits and gravy at a restaurant on the way to Royal Gorge. They passed through gorgeous Garden of the Gods, a natural formation of red rocks, on their way up in the mountains. When they arrived at the gorge, the extreme height took Adam's and Ashley's breath away. The three-mile, thirty-minute railway ride to the rim of the gorge wound through pines toward a breathtaking view—one that included several chipmunks and a deer.

Still, as they headed into Cripple Creek, both Ashley and Adam were restless, feeling like they had lost the opportunity to be involved in the hunt for the missing gold.

As the family wandered through the town of Cripple Creek, Adam and Ashley read aloud about its history from a brochure they had picked up.

"In 1891, after twelve years of searching, Bob Womack was the first to find gold in the gulch now known as Cripple Creek. The rush was on for what turned out to be the richest gold strike in the United States," read Adam.

"Within 10 years of the first strike," he continued, "there were 28 millionaires, 91 lawyers, 88 doctors, 41 assay offices, 3 railroads, and 70 saloons at Cripple Creek. By the end of the gold rush, roughly $432 million in gold had been mined in the area."

The Arlingtons visited the old Mollie-Kathleen gold mine, one of the few mines open to the public. When they were one thousand feet underground, each visitor on the tour was given a rock containing a small amount of gold. Looking at the shiny white specks of gold in the gray piece of ore, Adam understood what had drawn so many miners to the area more than a hundred years before.

As they exited the mine through the gift shop, the bright sun was blinding. What they saw next, however, was even more surprising. The black 4Runner! The short, stocky man from the tour was getting into the passenger side.

"Excuse me, sir!" Adam shouted. "Sir, please wait a minute!"

The stocky man looked back, furrowed a dark, thick eyebrow that seemed to cover both eyes, and jumped into the vehicle. It peeled out on the dirt road, much like it had the day before at Cave of the Winds. Ashley and Adam ran toward the vehicle with their shocked parents not far behind. They stopped at the edge of the parking lot as the 4Runner disappeared in the distance. Disappointed, they walked slowly back toward the gift shop.

"Excuse me, son, do you know that man?" the host of the Mollie-Kathleen gold mine tour asked.

"Sort of . . . but not really," Adam said. He turned and looked at the host, whose name tag said "Jack." "Do you know him?"

"No," Jack replied. "However, he did come up and ask about how we melted gold and what it was worth."

"What did you tell him?" Ashley asked.

"I said we don't do that here any longer and haven't for years," Jack said. "And besides, you don't do jobs off the street. I mean, people don't just show up with gold anymore and say, 'Here, cash me out,' as if it were poker chips being cashed in. Sure, in the old days the prospectors brought in their gold and got their money. But not today—it just doesn't work that way anymore."

"Did you notice anything special about the guy?" Adam asked.

"He mentioned the price of gold on the stock exchange, and he sounded like he was from the East Coast," Jack said. "He said 'New Yawk,' so I could tell he wasn't from around here."

The Arlingtons called the police, and ten minutes later a patrolman arrived at the mine. Adam and Ashley were ecstatic to see the patrolman, for now they could finally get an update on the case.

"From what I understand, you two have been very helpful," the patrolman said. Looking toward their parents, he added, "You should be proud of your children. They are obviously very bright."

"But what about the case?" Adam asked. "Do we have anything else new?"

"We?" the patrolman asked. "We, the police, are in the middle of an investigation. We don't give out that information to the general public. This case, should we move in a positive direction, will still have to go to trial. While we appreciate your help, we really can't include you in the investigation itself."

"We certainly understand that," Mrs. Arlington said, putting her arm around Adam.

The patrolman took the Arlingtons' statements, called in the new information, and left. Adam and Ashley briefly searched the ground around the mine entrance to find their souvenir pieces of ore, which they had dropped in the excitement of running after the black 4Runner.

"Did those guys do something wrong?" asked Jack when Adam and Ashley came back inside to find their parents.

"We don't know, but it sure looks that way," Ashley said. "They might've taken some gold from Cave of the Winds yesterday."

"You're kidding!" Jack said. "That's all over the news today!"

"Yeah, we know," Adam said, looking down, afraid that he wouldn't get another opportunity to help solve the crime.

"Oh, one more thing," the tour guide called out as Adam, Ashley, and their parents headed for the door. "The guy asked to use my phone when he was here. He said it was long distance, and I made him use the pay phone. Whoever he called might've been long distance, but I don't think it was out of state."

"How do you know that?" Ashley asked.

"Because I heard him say he wouldn't see whoever he was talking to again this week," Jack said. "He said they were in Mesa Verde at the start of the week, and they'd be clear at the other end of the state by the end of the week."

Adam quickly took his laptop out of his backpack and pulled up a map of Colorado. He saw that Mesa Verde National Park, with its historic Indian cliff dwellings of red clay, is in the southwest corner of Colorado, about twenty miles north of the New Mexico border. But the man's comment about the other end of the state raised as many questions as it could have possibly answered. Did he mean across the state to the north? If that was the case, the criminals could be headed up to Craig, the only big town in northwestern Colorado west of Steamboat Springs, a mountain ski resort. The only other area of note up there was Dinosaur National Monument, which was off the highway on the border with Utah, just twenty or so miles south of the Wyoming border.

If by "opposite" the man meant southeast, they could hide out in one of several small towns near the Kansas border and never be seen, especially if they laid low in the extraordinarily rural areas.

"Wait," Ashley said. "Maybe they meant the literal opposite. Mesa Verde is in the southwest corner of the state, right?"

"Right," replied Adam.

"Well, maybe they're going up to the northeast corner of the state, to Fort Morgan or Sterling," Ashley said, dragging her fingers across the atlas as she traced the possible route. "Really, the whole trip is interstate after they catch I-25. If they travel during the day, and especially if they travel during rush hour in Pueblo, Colorado Springs, and Denver, they could go virtually unnoticed."

"Do you think they'd risk being out in the open?" Adam asked.

"I'd rather do that than travel on state highways at night, where you are going to catch the eye of a state trooper sooner or later," Ashley said. "If there's only the state trooper and their 4Runner on a lonely highway, they're a lot more likely to be stopped than if they're cruising with hundreds or thousands of cars through busier areas on interstates. Plus, you can go so much faster on the interstate."

Ashley and Adam said good-bye to the tour guide and got in the SUV with their parents, who wanted to take the long way "home." That meant a scenic but long drive to Canon City and then east to Pueblo and north to Colorado Springs.

The family stopped to eat in Pueblo. Mr. Arlington called Deputy Martinez; after they talked for a minute, Ashley took the phone and relayed what they had found out from the Mollie-Kathleen tour guide.

"Thanks a lot," Martinez said. "I heard what you gave the patrolman. But this stuff about Mesa Verde might really be something. If they pay with credit cards or if anyone has a visual sighting, we might be able to pick up their trail and anticipate their next move. We're still looking for a needle in a haystack, but at least we have some more information. Thanks again, and tell your dad I want to get together before you leave Colorado even though I'm pretty tied up with this case."

Although Adam and Ashley wished they could follow the investigation some more, the next day promised to take them out of the loop, at least geographically.

It was really only a couple of miles out of the way. But those miles were straight up Pikes Peak.

An Initial Clue

The next morning, after a jog around the campground and down the adjacent hill, the family returned to the motor home to get cleaned up before leaving for the long trek up the mountain.

Ashley had just finished lacing up her hiking boots when the cell phone in the motor home rang. Her father answered.

"Hello, Paul," Mr. Arlington said. "Is everything all right?"

"Yes, sir, Alex, looking forward to seeing you!" Martinez told him. "I just want to ask Ashley or Adam something."

Her father passed the phone to Ashley.

"This is Deputy Martinez," he said. "How are you today?"

"I'm tired, and I'd rather talk to you about the case than hike up a mountain," Ashley said with a laugh.

"Ashley, do you and your brother still have your notes from the other day?" Deputy Martinez asked.

She looked at Adam and repeated the question; he nodded his head yes.

"We sure do," Ashley said.

"Good, can you stick around there? I can be by in twenty minutes," Deputy Martinez said.

Ashley checked with her father. It wasn't even 9:30, so they could spare the time. Plus, the mountain would be frigid at the peak at this time of the day. To help the police and see Paul, he said they could wait.

When Deputy Martinez arrived, he and Mr. Arlington exchanged a bear hug and then sat down to chat for a few minutes. After a while he, Ashley, and Adam went through their notes together.

"Does 'KY' mean anything to you two?" Martinez asked.

Ashley and Adam looked at each other and shook their heads no.

"Like a Kentucky license plate?" Ashley asked.

"That's a good guess, but we already checked that," Martinez said. "None of the cars in the Cave of the Winds parking lot that day had Kentucky plates. We monitored a transmission on the CB radio that may have been one of the thieves. He said that 'KY had to clear.' We're just trying to figure it out."

"Did any of the tourists have the initials KY?" Ashley asked.

Martinez went through his notes again.

"Not a single tourist with a K and a Y for both initials," he said. "One with a first name starting with K, another with a last name beginning with K, and one with the last name starting with Y. But none together."

Before leaving, Martinez commended Mr. and Mrs. Arlington for having such good kids.

"These kids do you a lot of credit, Alex, and your wife, too," he said to his old army friend. "Let's make time in the next few days to get together so I can get to know them better. I'll call you first chance I get."

"Do that," Mr. Arlington said. "We still have plenty to see in this state to keep us here; we aren't ready to head home yet!"

They said good-bye to the deputy and then loaded up the car for the trip up the mountain.

Pikes Peak didn't disappoint. Named after prospector Zebulon Pike, the mountain was chilly at the top, and snowcaps were still visible. The Arlingtons took one of the shorter hiking trails up the mountain, stopping often to admire the beautiful views.

When they reached the top, Mr. and Mrs. Arlington went to search for shirts in the gift shop. Adam and Ashley walked around outside.

"What do you make of this 'KY' thing?" Adam asked.

"I don't know," Ashley said as she strolled across the rocky dirt. "But I can't get it off my mind, either."

The Kentucky angle seemed illogical because there were no Kentucky license plates in the parking lot at the cave that day. A person's initials seemed to make the most sense, but it didn't match.

"Wait a minute," Adam said. "What if a husband's name starts with K and his wife's name starts with Y?"

"Hey," Ashley replied, "you might be on to something."

They flipped furiously through their notes but found nothing.

"You know, this might never be solved," Adam said as he flipped his notebook in the air. It landed by his feet, the pages turning in the wind. As he picked it up, his hand, wet from the condensation on his soft drink, moistened the page with the staff names on it.

"Oh no," Adam said. "Look what I've done now."

"That's OK, it's still readable," Ashley said. "See here: Kelly Yeardly, Tom Ramsay, Kevin Yarbrough, Rich Anderson, Kim Young, . . . Still legible."

Adam let out a whoop of pure excitement.

"What do Kelly Yeardly, Kevin Yarbrough, and Kim Young have in common?" he asked.

"Way to go, little bro," Ashley answered. "KY!" She quickly flipped open her cell phone and called Martinez.

"This is Deputy Martinez," the voice said after the call had been transferred.

Ashley explained about the initials.

"We just hit on that ourselves," Martinez said. "I don't know how we could have overlooked it. We're still in the process of checking everyone who was in the cave that day. I've got their work schedules; we'll follow up with them there or at their homes."

"Great," Ashley said. "Good luck." She and Adam already had the wheels in their minds cranked up to 100 miles an hour.

"Do you think it was the man?" Adam said. "Or the young woman, or even the girl?"

"I don't think it was the girl," Ashley said. "She's about my age. She just seemed too young to be involved with something like this."

At the same time, they couldn't rule any of the three out. They knew nothing except the names and ages of the three staff members, all of whom had the initials KY.

"There's an easy solution to mysteries like this, you know," Ashley told her brother.

"What's that?" Adam asked.

"Don't hire three people with the same initials!" Ashley said as they both laughed.

Their mother and father, looking like the ultimate tourists, came out of the gift shop wearing their new Pikes Peak sweatshirts.

"What do you think, kids?" their mom asked.

"Looks great, Mom," Ashley answered. "Dad, that sweatshirt looks really good on you. But if you want it to look even better, you should cut the tags off."

Their father looked at the tags and shrugged. He didn't care, and he couldn't reach the tags. Besides, he wasn't making a fashion statement. Nonetheless, he let his wife cut off the tags.

"What were you two laughing about when we came out?" Mrs. Arlington asked.

"Just a joke, Mom," Adam answered. On the way to the car he and Ashley explained what had happened in the short time that their parents had been shopping.

"Kids," Mr. Arlington said, "I haven't been altogether comfortable with your involvement in this from the start. And now, I'm growing more uncomfortable. You might be on to something with this 'KY' thing. If one or more of the staff members *is* involved, they might remember you from the cave that day. These thieves could be dangerous people, and I don't want you anywhere near them."

"Dad, you heard Deputy Martinez, right?" Adam asked. "Do you think he'd let us anywhere near the police investigation?"

That was a good point—one Mr. Arlington decided to pursue that evening. After the family descended the peak and pulled into a restaurant for a late afternoon meal, he waited in the car, dialed the cell phone, and reached Paul Martinez just as he was about to leave his office.

"Paul, I'm concerned about my kids' safety," he began.

"I certainly understand that," Deputy Martinez said. "And please believe that their safety is more important to me than recovering the gold. When I pass along information, I don't pass along the source. Their names are only in my auxiliary notes within a sealed computer file at my home. No one at the office can access it."

"I appreciate that," Mr. Arlington said. "Anne and I have tried to teach our kids to be responsible and to help people whenever they can. But we're still their parents, and we don't want them to get hurt."

"With the way those kids are, you and Anne are obviously very good parents," Martinez said. "I'm a parent too, Alex, so I understand how you feel."

"Thanks very much," Mr. Arlington said, and hung up with a promise to talk again soon. Even after talking to Martinez, though, he still had an uneasy feeling in the pit of his stomach.

The Puzzling Professor

The Arlingtons had planned an overnight trip to north-ern Colorado the next night. As Mr. and Mrs. Arlington talked about the trip that evening, they worried about giv-ing their children too much freedom, especially with everything that had happened. Going to northern Col-orado, however, meant the kids would be far away from the investigation. The family agreed to ride together to Denver, where Mr. and Mrs. Arlington would visit old friends, the Allens, who had lived near them in D.C. for several years before moving to Colorado. The family would meet again in Greeley, just an hour or so northeast of Den-ver, when midafternoon rolled around.

They woke up the next morning, packed a couple of days' worth of clothes, took a morning run through surprisingly chilly summer air, and then headed north on I-25. As they drove through Denver on the interstate, Adam marveled at Mile High Stadium, where he had seen John Elway on television so many times as Elway worked his magic for the Denver Broncos. Just across the street from the stadium was McNichol's Arena, the home of the Denver Nuggets and Colorado Avalanche. Not far off the interstate to the east sat Coors Field, home to the Colorado Rockies baseball team.

As Adam and Ashley dropped off their parents, the kids suggested a change in plans.

"Mom, Dad, instead of visiting the Colorado History Museum, can Adam and I go to the University of Colorado and see that basketball coach we met at Cave of the Winds?" Ashley asked.

"That is, 'May Adam and I,' and yes, I think that would be fine," Mrs. Arlington said with a smile.

The ride to Boulder went pretty quickly. Adam and Ashley found the Coors Events/Conference Center, where the women's and men's basketball teams played. Then they walked to the stadium and looked up the women's basketball office. The head coach was a woman, but she wasn't the coach they had seen that day in the cave. Ashley looked at pictures of the staff on a wall. Tim Timmons was the coach she had seen. They searched the directory and found Timmons's office number. It was almost noon when they knocked at his door, finding a darkened office with two figures sitting in it.

"Come on in," a man said, rising to turn on the lights and introducing himself as Timmons. There was another assistant coach in the room. The two were viewing tapes of high school seniors that they might recruit in the future.

"Do you remember me?" Ashley asked. "I saw you at . . ."

"Cave of the Winds three days ago," Timmons said. "Sure, I remember you. Boy, that was quite a day, wasn't it?"

"You're telling me," Ashley answered with a smile.

Introductions followed, and Adam and Ashley got a tour of the campus courtesy of Coach Timmons. Ashley also worked out for him, playing a little one-on-one against Adam. She then took on Timmons, a former small-college player, and held her own against him. He asked for Ashley's high school back in D.C. and her coach's name.

"I'll follow you this year," Timmons said. "You might have a shot at playing here, or at least at the Division I level. You're tall enough, and you certainly can dribble and shoot. You stay in touch, and feel free to look around the campus more if you'd like. Most of the buildings are open, and any professors who are here could answer your questions."

Ashley and Adam went to the chemistry building across the campus. Only a receptionist was in the main office. Phyllis was very talkative and provided plenty of information about the chemistry program at the University of Colorado. Ashley would get an adviser and, as a chemistry major, would have priority on getting departmental classes over students who weren't chemistry majors.

"Thanks," Ashley said as she and Adam shook Phyllis's hand. As they walked out the door, they stopped to look at the faculty pictures on the wall. Photos of nearly twenty CU professors were arranged in the shape of a diamond.

"Look at this guy, Ash," Adam said, pointing to a man with a squarish head and a thick beard that grew from the bottom of his neck to nearly his eyes. "He looks like he should be teaching about cavemen!"

Ashley looked at the picture and started to smile. But her jaw dropped when she saw the photo above that picture.

"No way!" Ashley shrieked. "It's HIM!"

Dr. Kevin Yarbrough was pictured, looking just the same as he had at Cave of the Winds, minus the cave's staff shirt he had been wearing when he nervously came out of the gift shop to answer the officer's questions that day. Phyllis came running out of the office.

"Is everyone all right?" she asked.

"This man, where is his office?" Ashley asked, pointing to the picture.

"Oh dear," Phyllis said. "That picture shouldn't even be up there. We had planned to hire Dr. Yarbrough about a month ago, but a reference turned up a problem; I think it was a criminal conviction."

"For what?" Ashley asked.

"You know, dear, I'm not really sure," Phyllis replied. "All I know is that he didn't check out. Let me get the keys to this case. His picture should come down."

"Where did he teach before here?" Ashley asked.

"He never did teach here," Phyllis said. "But he had a long history in Colorado, if I recall. Then he left and went overseas for a while. This was going to be what he came back for."

"Do you know where he went from Colorado?" Ashley asked.

"Never heard a word," Phyllis answered. "I know he had been in New York for quite a while. Oh, you wouldn't believe how strong an accent the man had. It was almost hard to understand him sometimes. But he didn't talk much, if I recall."

The accent! Another piece of the puzzle was sliding into place. Adam and Ashley looked at each other, and Ashley winked. It seemed highly likely that Kevin Yarbrough was the "KY" involved in the crime.

Ashley called Deputy Martinez, but he wasn't in the office. Then she and Adam headed toward the student center to get a soda.

"Can you believe it was that man?" Adam asked.

"Well, yes and no," Ashley replied. "On the one hand, no, because he seemed so nice and gentle behind the gift shop counter, not a care in the world. On the other hand, yes, because it's kind of hard to imagine a guy who is in his forties working at a place like a gift shop."

Adam looked through his notes. He wondered what the connection was between the guy in the 4Runner and Kevin Yarbrough, and asked Ashley why the two men had committed the crime in broad daylight.

"Well, I don't think it's like a shoe store, where they give just about all the employees a set of keys to the office," Ashley said. "They probably couldn't get access to the cave after dark. Plus, I don't think their 'lost child' diversion worked as well as they thought it would. If Jim hadn't come out of the office, the authorities would not have known anything until much later. Actually, it was a pretty good plan."

Adam agreed but still wanted to establish a concrete link between Kevin Yarbrough and the crime. And both Ashley and Adam wondered how many other people were involved. At least the driver, the stocky man on the tour, and Yarbrough—so no fewer than three. But how did they know each other? Where were they from? How did they find out about the gold crystals? And how did they get the gold crystals out without being noticed?

"So many questions," Adam said as he shook his head back and forth. "And almost no answers."

Ashley patted him on the back. Nestled against the mountains, CU was set in the most picturesque of places. College students with backpacks slung over one shoulder mingled about, talking about summer school classes and the chances CU's football team had to excel in the fall season, which was just around the corner.

"Let's try Deputy Martinez again," Adam said.

Ashley made the call. This time, Deputy Martinez was in the office. After a short delay, she was transferred to his extension. Another deputy answered but confirmed that Deputy Martinez was nearby and would be with her in a moment.

"This is Deputy Martinez," he soon said.

"Hi," Ashley said. "This is Ashley Arlington."

"Hello, Ashley," Martinez said. "I bet you know about Kevin Yarbrough by now. Or do you?"

"We sure do," Ashley said.

"Yeah, me too," Martinez said. "We checked out Kim Young and Kelly Yeardly, and they're clean. Actually, Kelly saw Yarbrough talking to the man you saw getting into the 4Runner."

"So, did you know Yarbrough was supposed to teach at CU?" Ashley asked.

"No," Martinez said. "What is that all about? Where are you?"

"Adam and I are at the University of Colorado in Boulder," Ashley said. She recapped the events that had taken place in the chemistry department.

"I'll be!" Martinez said. "So, this guy knew a bit about chemistry."

"Obviously, he knew quite a bit," Ashley said. "He was set to be a full-fledged faculty member, but a final reference didn't check out."

"And that reference was . . . ?" Martinez asked.

"Can't find that out, although the secretary in the chem department said she thought it was a criminal conviction," Ashley said. "When Adam and I asked for more information, she just didn't have it. That might be one you have to track down."

"There had to be some kind of screening process and a search committee as well," Martinez said. "I'll get in touch with the search director or the department chair. I'll subpoena their records if I have to."

"Good luck," Ashley said. "If we find anything out, we'll be in touch."

"Be careful, you two," Martinez said. "I'm concerned about your involvement. At the same time, you've really helped. Just be smart, okay?"

"You got it, Deputy," Ashley said. "Good-bye."

A Run-in with the 4Runner

Adam and Ashley returned to the parking lot at the Events Center. Although it was only midafternoon, they were eager to get to their motel in Greeley. Mr. and Mrs. Arlington had told them they'd be there early in the afternoon, so there would be time to do something together as a family. Adam and Ashley knew that meant a lot to their parents.

Adam drove, making his way back to I-25 and heading north. With so many Denver radio stations to choose from, the pair just cranked up the music and the cruise control, settling on 70 miles an hour. Aside from the SUV pulling slightly to the right with the strong wind out of the west, the drive was relaxing. Adam and Ashley soon exited on U.S. 34 east to Greeley.

As they pulled up to the motel exit, Adam was cut off.

"Adam, look out!" Ashley screamed.

Adam hit his brakes hard to avoid a collision with a driver who was obviously in a big hurry.

"We're all right, Ash," Adam said. "We're all right. I'll just hang back and give this guy some room."

Adam and Ashley both instinctively looked at the vehicle that had cut them off. Perhaps they could get the license number and turn the guy in.

"New York plates?" Adam said in wonder.

Ashley looked closer.

"A black 4Runner—Adam, it's them!" Ashley yelled.

The 4Runner's driver had no idea that he was being followed by someone who knew who he was, or at least what he had done. He headed north on U.S. 85, which would ultimately lead to Cheyenne, Wyoming, after passing through several small towns in Colorado.

Adam followed the 4Runner north. As they passed through Greeley and went to a four-lane road, Ashley got the license number—RD-3042.

She wrote it down as Adam tried to pull alongside the vehicle to get a look at who was driving. But the driver was going fast—well over the speed limit. Adam sped up to 75 miles an hour, which just enabled Ashley to identify the man in the passenger seat as the stocky man who was in front of her on the tour, the man who had worn the denim jacket with the sleeves cut off at the shoulders. The driver was harder to see, but it definitely was not Kevin Yarbrough. As Adam tried to keep up and inched closer to the driver's side, the driver of the 4Runner figured out he was being followed. He sped up and left Adam and Ashley far behind.

"Slow down, Adam," Ashley said, and Adam began to ease his assault on the gas pedal.

"I know," Adam said. "We'll just try to keep him in sight."

The road narrowed to two lanes, and the 4Runner passed cars, pickups, and semitrailers as though it was a train steaming down a track. Adam kept his eyes on the 4Runner but was losing ground fast. The cars and trucks the 4Runner had passed weren't even going 70, much less the 90 or more the 4Runner was doing.

Four cars exited in the small town of Eaton. Just a couple of miles up the road in Ault, the Arlingtons finally made up most of the ground they had lost, closing in on the 4Runner as it neared Ault's only stoplight. The light had turned red as both vehicles approached. A semitrailer was coming from the east, so the 4Runner would have to stop before moving forward.

Off to the right Adam saw a train coming south down the tracks. When the crossing arm was down, it would stop eastbound traffic on State Highway 14. The train would force the 4Runner to turn back to the interstate or continue straight ahead. If it went back to the interstate, Adam and Ashley could call the authorities, who would catch him as easily as catching fish in a barrel. If the 4Runner went straight, it would be no better off because there were not many places to turn off between Ault and the Wyoming border.

Ashley tried to call the police on her cell phone but was unable to get a clear signal. She quickly got out of the vehicle and headed for the outside pay phone at the convenience store at the southwest corner of the intersection.

At that moment, just before the train reached the intersection, the 4Runner plowed through the warning bar, knocking the hunk of red-and-white striped metal up in the air. Adam called to Ashley.

"Get back in here!" Adam yelled. "He's going!"

Ashley didn't turn. The train was sounding its horn as the 4Runner's driver risked life and limb to beat the train across the tracks and turn east on State Highway 14. As Adam pulled into the parking lot of the convenience store, Ashley was talking to the police.

Shouting into the receiver, Ashley told the police to contact Deputy Martinez in Colorado Springs. By then there had already been an all-points bulletin issued for the vehicle and its occupants.

By the time the train cleared the intersection, the 4Runner could not be seen. A coal train had to slow to 20 miles an hour to pass through town. This train creaked along even more slowly, taking a good twelve minutes or so, Adam guessed. That gave the 4Runner enough time to be on the way to Sterling. Sterling was at the opposite end of the state from Mesa Verde, one of the options the Arlingtons had considered after talking to the tour guide at the Mollie-Kathleen mine. If the vehicle didn't head to Sterling, there were several roads that would lead it to Nebraska or Kansas in only a few hours.

"Let's go for the interstate, Ash," Adam said excitedly. "We could beat them to I-80."

"And then do what?" Ashley asked. "Adam, we're doing the right thing, helping the police. But a high-speed chase? No. Even if we caught up to them, then what? They shoot us? They run us off the road? They pull a gun and steal our car? Let's head back to Greeley."

Adam was disappointed. He had seen so many action movies that he thought the good guys really did always win, and without getting hurt. But Ashley was right, and Adam knew it.

They drove south toward Greeley. The drive that had seemed to take only minutes a while earlier took almost a half hour. They pulled into the motel parking lot in Greeley and found their room. Ashley called Deputy Martinez as Adam filled his parents in on what had happened.

Deputy Martinez said that despite the valiant effort by the Arlingtons, the suspects had not been spotted, although roadblocks had been set up on all state highways leaving northeastern Colorado to Nebraska and Kansas, as well as one by I-25 and one on U.S. 85, just in case the 4Runner had turned around at some point and back-tracked. Authorities in neighboring states had also been alerted.

The plate checks had come back on the cars that had been in the parking lot of Cave of the Winds the day of the theft. The car from New Jersey checked out fine, as did one of the two cars from New York. The other car from New York, however, was stolen. It seemed likely that someone on the tour had been involved with the theft and had slipped through the fingers of authorities at the time of the crime.

"We almost had them!" Adam complained to Ashley and his parents.

"We?" asked his father.

"You know what I mean, Dad," Adam said.

"And you know what I mean," his father said, looking over his glasses at his son. "You had absolutely no business driving so fast or following such dangerous men. You and your sister could have been seriously hurt, or you could have hurt someone else. You made a bad decision, Adam. No more driving for you for the rest of the trip."

"Yes, sir," Adam said, looking at the floor. He didn't know which felt worse, disappointing his father or failing to catch the 4Runner.

A Hot Tip from Old News

The family went to Fort Morgan the following morning. It was a pretty day on Colorado's eastern plains, but Adam and Ashley were almost sick over missing what seemed to be a golden chance to catch the criminals.

After stopping in downtown Fort Morgan, a quaint town just off Interstate 76, the family headed south to the town of Limon. Adam spotted a small store along the highway and convinced the rest of the family to stop for a break. Paying for bottles of water and orange juice, he made small talk with the clerk as he reached into his pocket for a couple of dollars and some change.

"You work yesterday?" Adam asked.

"From 10:00 A.M. to midnight—it was awful," said the clerk, a young man in his early twenties. "We're short staffed, so that's how it is for a while."

"You didn't happen to see a 4Runner from New York pull in here, did you?" Adam asked the clerk.

"Not that I recall," the clerk answered. "Someone you know?"

"No, not really," Adam replied.

As Adam pushed open the door and stepped outside, the clerk waved him back.

"Wait a minute, there was a black thing that looked like one of those sport utility vehicles, but I'm not sure that it was a 4Runner," the clerk said. "I mean, both guys in it weren't in the best shape. One of them was wearing a jean jacket that had no sleeves—the only reason I remember that is because it had dirt just ground in on the shoulders. They could have been from New York, I guess."

"Did they pay with a check or credit card?" Adam asked.

"No, I don't think they got anything," the clerk said. "They just stopped to use our bathrooms, and I thought it was rude that they didn't say thanks or anything, and they didn't buy anything."

Adam motioned to his parents to wait a minute. He called Deputy Martinez, who was out of the office again. Adam was transferred to the deputy's voice mail and left a detailed message, even giving him the store's phone number and address from the register receipt. He also relayed what the clerk had told him.

"What was that all about?" his mother asked when he got in the car.

Adam knew his parents would be upset if he told them that he was still on the trail and that it was getting warm once again. At the same time, he had never lied to his parents and didn't want to start now. So, after thinking about it for just a few seconds, he told them what had happened.

His parents said nothing, perhaps respecting his honesty just as much as they worried over his obsession with the case. Ashley smiled at him, proud of his detective work.

"What did Deputy Martinez say?" Ashley asked.

"Got his voice mail, so I just left a message," Adam answered.

Over the next two days, it appeared the Arlingtons' involvement in the case had come to an end after an eventful week.

Once again, however, appearances were misleading.

In Limon, the family had picked up a copy of the local weekly paper, the *Limon Leader*. Reading a local paper in each town gave the family a chance to keep up with current events and, too, it showed what was important to that area's residents and what was happening in town. In fact, the family used weekly newspapers from different towns during most of their trips to catch events like county fairs and local art exhibits.

Limon housed a state prison. The prison, while not welcomed by everyone in town, was really good for Limon's economy because it brought jobs. Being on the eastern plains, Limon didn't have as much to offer as some of the mountain communities, except that it was easily accessible because of Interstate 70. Still, many of the town's residents didn't like the prison or see a real need for it. There had been a heated debate on that topic at a town council meeting the week before the Arlingtons' arrival, according to a front page article in that Tuesday's edition of the newspaper, which was already several days old.

"Look at this headline next to the town council story," Adam said. "No wonder some of the town's residents don't like having the prison in the area."

"Dangerous Felons Still at Large after State Prison Breakout" the headline announced.

Adam read part of the story out loud, "Four felons escaped from the maximum security Limon State Prison late last week. . . . Two of the felons were caught within hours of the 2:00 A.M. breakout. However, the other two men are still at large. They were from . . . New York!" Adam declared. Mug shots of the men appeared on the front page of the paper.

"That guy—it says his name is Robert Brookholder—was the man driving the 4Runner, and the other one, Bill Thomas, was the man in the denim jacket who left the cave that day!" Ashley said. They called Deputy Martinez, who hadn't connected the breakout at Limon with the gold theft. Martinez grabbed a copy of the circular with Bill Thomas's and Robert Brookholder's names and mug shots on it, which had been passed out at the deputies' meeting earlier that week.

"There might be a reward in this after all," Martinez said to Ashley. "Maybe one for the prison breakout and another if we recover the gold crystals."

"We really don't expect any money," Ashley said. "I don't know if our parents would let us accept it, anyway, just for doing the right thing. If we did get a reward, we'd have to donate it to a good charity."

The fact that the driver of the 4Runner, Brookholder, had escaped from Limon and still had the guts to pass back through the area after being chased through Ault frightened Adam and Ashley. According to the story in the *Leader,* Brookholder hadn't been convicted of any violent crimes, but had so many burglary and fraud convictions that he had had the book thrown at him after his most recent trial. Brookholder had jumped bail from New York on felony burglary charges and had been convicted in Denver of a robbery charge. He escaped while serving a ten-to-fifteen-year sentence and was awaiting extradition to New York.

"Now do you see why it's so important to let the police do the investigating?" Mr. Arlington asked. "There are trained law enforcement officers handling this case. They have the means to defend themselves and the law behind them to back up any action they take."

"Got it, Dad," Ashley said.

"Ten-four," Adam said with a smile, teasing his suddenly solemn father into a grin.

The *Leader* story also contained background information about Bill Thomas. A petty convict at first, Thomas had plenty of experience with metal—he was either stealing it or spending time behind it. Thomas was involved in several jewelry store robberies, although no one had ever been injured. Thomas was a native of New York, but he had deep ties to Colorado. A sister, Janet Thomas, lived in Gunnison, a mountain community that was home to Western State College. Thomas also had an uncle, Thad Banks, in Alamosa, located near La Veta Pass in the mountains of southern Colorado.

Alamosa, Adam thought, *that rings a bell.* During an orientation with various colleges in the spring semester of his sophomore year, Adam had heard of Adams State College.

The teachers at Thomas Jefferson High School had passed out cards, and the students had chosen two possible college majors. Adam had picked computer programming and teaching. Adams State College had had a representative there. Although Adam did not remember much about the woman from ASC, he had known that his family was planning to visit Colorado that summer. The woman suggested he stop by for a tour of the campus should he be in town.

"We're all going to Trinidad tomorrow with the Allens," Mr. Arlington told Ashley and Adam. "We're going to see the Old Baca House and Pioneer Museum. It's a state historical monument."

"Dad, we want to visit a couple of colleges," Adam said.

Ashley looked at Adam with her head tilted to the side. "We do?" Ashley asked.

"Yes," Adam said, staring hard at his sister, "we do."

"Oh yes," Ashley said. "I remember now."

Adam talked about visiting Adams State College and, time permitting, Western State College in Gunnison.

"I'll make sure that the Allens don't mind driving to Trinidad," Mr. Arlington said. "Ashley, you can drive the SUV, and we'll all meet back at the motor home tomorrow night."

The kids nodded their heads in agreement. Adam and Ashley went outside, sitting under the camper's awning. The sun had set, and a cool breeze nipped at their noses. Ashley wore a red and white windbreaker and jeans; Adam wore a sweatsuit and a guilty look.

"What are we doing tomorrow, for real?" Ashley asked.

"We really are visiting colleges—I wouldn't lie to Mom and Dad," Adam said. "But there is a little bit more to the story that I didn't think was worth mentioning," he said sheepishly.

Adam filled her in on his plan to investigate Bill Thomas's relatives. They headed into the motor home to sleep for the night. Adam, feeling restless, played on his computer while Ashley put on some earphones and let her new CD put her to sleep.

Too Close for Comfort

The next morning was overcast. Gray clouds appeared to be stacked in the mile-high sky like building blocks. Sleet moistened the grass, but the windows of the motor home weren't covered with rain.

"Listen, you two," Mrs. Arlington said to Adam and Ashley. "The roads will be slippery in the mountains. When you go up La Veta Pass, assume that the roads are going to be slick and that other drivers aren't aware of it. So use extra caution."

Ashley agreed. She would do the driving that day. Her brother's excursion into the high-speed range while chasing the 4Runner had knocked him out of the driver's seat. They headed south on Interstate 25 to Pueblo. They drove past the exit to Royal Gorge once again and stopped to eat in Salida after being on the road for nearly two hours. Poncha Pass was at 9,010 feet, similar to the 9,413-foot La Veta Pass they would take coming back. Ashley deftly negotiated the roads through Monarch Pass at 11,312 feet above sea level. The roads were wet, but the truck drivers were cautious, making the trip longer but actually more enjoyable. Ashley and Adam marveled at the mountains and how the trees stood straight up, even on the steepest of slopes.

Gunnison was beautiful, nestled in a valley with peaks visible in almost every direction. Adam had already found Janet Thomas's address in an on-line phone directory. He and Ashley headed to her house in a subdivision just outside of town.

The house was a nice wooden bi-level home, pretty big for just one person, Ashley thought.

"Let's knock on the door," Adam said.

"And say what?" Ashley responded.

"I don't know," Adam said. "But we didn't come all this way just to stop and look."

Ashley parked in front of the house, and she and Adam went to the front door. They knocked, waited, and knocked again. No one answered.

"Now what?" Ashley asked as she and Adam walked back to the car.

"I was hoping you'd have an idea," he replied.

They drove down the block, made a right turn, and stopped at a convenience store. An older woman was talking to the clerk when Adam and Ashley went inside. Adam saw an opportunity that he couldn't pass up.

"You two live around here?" Adam asked.

Both the young man working at the store and the older woman nodded wordlessly.

"Actually," Ashley chipped in, "we're a little lost. We spoke to Janet Thomas not long ago about someone she knew who could rent us a place if we end up coming to college here."

"Goodness," the older woman said. "You must have talked to her a while ago. She just got married and won't be back for another three weeks."

"Oh," Ashley said. "Thanks a lot."

"But we do have these free real estate and rental guides," the clerk said, pulling one from a newsstand. "Here, you two can have one."

"Thanks," Ashley said. She and Adam picked up a couple of sodas and paid for them.

"Thanks for your help," Adam said.

"You'll have to catch Janet sometime in late July," the older woman said.

"Yeah," the clerk added. "She's really a nice woman. She was thrilled to get out of here, especially since her loony brother escaped from prison over in Limon."

They know! Adam thought.

"Her brother is a prisoner?" he asked, acting as if he didn't know.

"Yes, but she has nothing to do with him," the clerk said. "She's estranged from the whole family—I guess they are all more like her brother than they are like her. She said she hasn't talked to him in twenty years. We'd have never known about it, but the police poked around up here when he first escaped."

"Well," Adam said, opening the door for Ashley, "thanks for everything."

Adam and Ashley drove to Western State College and walked around the campus, talking to students they met and learning as much about the school as they could. Although the trip had yielded little information, it did close the door on Gunnison as far as the case was involved. Ashley and Adam decided to start back toward Alamosa. On the way they headed down to La Jara, catching a ride on the Cumbres and Toltec Scenic Railroad before heading north to Pikes Stockade, a state historical monument. The time together was a good break for Adam and Ashley. They talked about one day living in Colorado, a state to which they were growing quite attached.

"I could live in the mountains," Adam said. "Give me a cabin at 13,000 feet and a hookup for my computer, and call me on holidays."

Ashley laughed.

"I'll be in Boulder," she said. "There's plenty to do in Boulder and more in Denver. You can come visit."

"So can you, Ash," Adam said with a smile.

The pair headed to Alamosa. Adam had already found a downtown address for Thad Banks. They looked for Second Street, but didn't see the street sign until they were already in the intersection. They decided to turn around at Third Street and come back to Second Street.

"Wait," Adam said, pointing. "There's an alley. It would be faster to cut through there."

Ashley turned down the narrow road, which was moist from the day's rain. They got halfway down the alley and saw two cars parked behind a house. The cars blocked the road just enough that the SUV wouldn't fit through the small opening.

"Be careful backing up," Adam said. "This alley is really narrow."

"Wait a minute," Adam said, and Ashley pushed down hard on the brakes. "Doesn't that car look familiar?"

The dirty little compact vehicle did look familiar. They pulled a bit closer.

"That's Kevin Yarbrough's car from Cave of the Winds!" Adam proclaimed.

"You know, I think you're right," Ashley said, looking toward the back window of the gray house where the cars were parked. A big wooden fence gave the house a lot of privacy. It also gave Adam and Ashley a chance to get a better look at the cars. They pulled out their notebooks.

"That other car, read me the plate number," Adam said to Ashley.

Ashley couldn't see the other car clearly. It was also dirty and was parked at an angle that blocked its front plate from plain view.

"I'll have to pull around and come back down the other end of the alley," Ashley said. She shifted into reverse and quietly backed out the way she had entered the alley. They drove around the block and came down the other side. They still couldn't see the plate through the dirt, so Adam got out.

Ashley looked in her notes where she had written BAT-101, N.Y. That could be the stolen car that didn't check out. Deputy Martinez had said that one car from New York and the one from New Jersey had been cleared, but the other New York car had been stolen.

Adam hopped back in the car, drawing the passenger door closed as silently as possible.

"BAT-101," he said.

"Bingo!" Ashley replied.

The two backed down the other side of the alley and pulled into the parking lot of a McDonald's. Ashley called Deputy Martinez, who contacted the authorities in Alamosa as well as the state patrol.

"What should we do?" Ashley asked Martinez on the phone.

"You two need to get as far away from there as possible!" Martinez said urgently. "Right now!"

"But what if this turns into something?" Ashley asked.

"Yes, Ashley, what if it does?" Martinez asked. "There are probably two convicted felons in that house, both on the run from authorities. What does an animal do when it is wounded or trapped?"

"It fights like it's fighting for its life," Ashley answered.

"Yes," the deputy said. "I appreciate your help. Now get out of there! I'll be in touch tomorrow or the day after."

"Okay, good-bye," Ashley said.

Sirens wailed in the background. Adam and Ashley, thinking they'd be safe at the restaurant, decided to stay put, have some lunch, and listen. They sat out in the parking lot and rolled down the windows in the SUV. The sirens were coming closer.

"What I wouldn't give for a police scanner right now," Adam moaned.

Just then, the small compact car sped by on the road in front of them, followed closely by a pair of Alamosa police cruisers. Before it could negotiate the next intersection, a state patrol vehicle pulled out in front of it. The small compact swerved and hit the curb, flipping onto its top and skidding into a fire hydrant at the corner. Water sprayed fiercely into the car as a man who looked like Thomas struggled to free himself.

Thomas did manage to work his way out of the car, but his freedom was short-lived. The police converged on him from all sides.

"Hands up—now!" one of the Alamosa police officers shouted, his gun drawn and pointed at Thomas.

"Give me the other hand!" the state patrolman yelled, pulling Thomas's left arm behind his back and handcuffing him. The Arlington kids could hear no more of the dialogue as the shouting and yelling ended. By the time a tow truck showed up for Thomas's car, the Alamosa fire department had shut off the water main. With Thomas long gone in the back of a police car, Adam and Ashley walked closer to the small compact. The windows were all broken out, except for a small rear one on the passenger side of the two-door hatchback.

There was definitely no gold in the back of the vehicle. But a policeman searching it found a handgun and a sawed-off shotgun. Their parents and Deputy Martinez were right; whoever these criminals were, they were playing for keeps.

Half a Pack of Thieves

The pair was very quiet as Ashley steered them down La Veta Pass. The sight of guns had brought home their father's point that crime-solving was not a game.

The pair wound down La Veta Pass and stopped in Walsenburg for hot chocolate.

"Adam, I don't know what to do," Ashley said. "I mean, I think we've really helped, but I also think Dad is right."

Adam didn't want to agree but pointed out that they had been cautious, almost too cautious at times in his mind.

"We have a chance to help solve one of the biggest crimes of the summer," Adam said. "As long as we stay smart, we'll be fine."

Ashley smiled at her brother's attitude. This was the same self-confidence that had led him to run for and win the office of student body president as a sophomore. All of their accomplishments had come from hard work and from trying to do the right thing. If Adam believed in what they were doing that much, maybe she should too.

Ashley called Deputy Martinez, who was filled with good news.

"They didn't just get Thomas, they got Yarbrough, too," Martinez beamed into the phone. "This is a big break for this case. With these two in custody we have it half solved!"

"Have they said anything?" Ashley asked.

"No, but they kept asking how we found them," Martinez said with a laugh. "I never did tell the state patrol or Alamosa P.D. who gave me the tip. I just told them it was an anonymous caller. The police down there are just on cloud nine. They think the two guys were planning to hit a bank down there because they found a bunch of notes that had its hours, number of workers at closing time, a layout of the bank—those kinds of things. Regardless of how much closer this puts us to the gold crystals, we might have already prevented an even more violent crime. You two are heroes."

Ashley could hear noise in the background on Martinez's end of the line.

"Hey, call me back in an hour or two," he said. "They're bringing Thomas in here now."

They were still forty-five minutes from Pueblo, and then almost another hour from their campground north of Colorado Springs.

Ashley hung up the phone and looked at Adam with a big grin.

She relayed the story about the bank heist being prevented and that Yarbrough had also been caught.

"You're right," Ashley said. "We're doing the right thing."

Almost ninety minutes had passed as they rolled into Colorado Springs, so Ashley went downtown to the El Paso Sheriff's Department. They asked at the reception counter to speak with Deputy Martinez. After producing her driver's license, Ashley was told it would be just a minute.

Martinez came out into the lobby.

"We should check out some badges for you two," Martinez said with a smile as he shook hands with Ashley and Adam.

The deputy took them back to his office. It was small, but well organized. A shade covered a window no bigger than two feet by two feet.

"Well, we've interviewed both men," Martinez said. "Yarbrough won't say a word. That makes sense, because he has the least to gain—and the most to lose—by admitting anything."

"Did he say anything about the University of Colorado?" Ashley asked.

"We mentioned it to him, and he just shrugged his shoulders without answering," Martinez said. "He's definitely smarter than Thomas. We did track down the information he provided to the university when he was almost hired by the chemistry department. He is a native New Yorker. He went to top schools for his graduate work and appeared to have the world at his feet. He taught chemistry at three Colorado high schools, then took a job teaching at a state college in New York. He had it all, including a wife and two children. Then about ten years ago, his wife left him, taking the kids, and he supposedly hasn't heard from her since. At least that's what his ex-wife told us when we called her this afternoon.

"That might have freaked him out. He got nailed in the divorce, had to pay child support and alimony. He was forced to sell their house in the divorce decree. He did some work for a precious mineral company overseas and made a boatload of money. Then he came back and started a phony investment scheme in Colorado. Funny thing is, he probably could've lived off what he had brought back with him, as far as money was concerned. The investment scheme collapsed, and the Feds were down his throat faster than you could make change for a dollar.

"He served five years and was hit with a pretty big fine. He got out and worked odd jobs before settling into a small apartment in Cripple Creek."

"Cripple Creek?" Adam asked. "There's gold out there. Was he involved in any of the mining in that area?"

"It doesn't appear so, at least not yet," Martinez said. "He lived like a hermit from what we can tell. No one in Cripple Creek has said they knew him."

"What about Thomas?" Ashley asked. "And what were the two of them doing in Alamosa?"

"Well, from what I can tell, you two pretty much figured out that they were staying with Thomas's uncle," Martinez said. "Thomas was raised in New York and has only two family connections here in Colorado, the sister in Gunnison, who wants nothing to do with him, and an older uncle who gave him shelter but knew little about what Thomas was up to."

"Any clue on how Thomas and Yarbrough knew each other?" Adam asked.

"That part of the mystery has been solved," Martinez said. "They did time together in Limon. They only spent about three months together, but apparently they became pretty good friends. Thomas also met Brookholder in prison, and as you know, they eventually broke out together. We can't connect Yarbrough directly to Brookholder yet; although they both served time at Limon, they didn't serve time together. But it's a logical guess that they met through their mutual friend Thomas.

"I don't know if Brookholder and the other guy in the 4Runner are leaving these guys out to dry or what. Except for a few guns, these guys had nothing, just a couple of dirty, cheap cars and no place to hide. I'm guessing those two guys in the 4Runner are trying to unload the gold as we speak."

There was a knock at the door. Martinez opened it just a crack, not to be rude, but because there was not enough room unless Ashley and Adam stood up.

"It's Thomas," the deputy said to Martinez. "He said he wants to talk."

Martinez told the Arlingtons they could go now.

"No way," Adam said. "We want to hear what he tells you."

"Adam, you and your sister probably deserve to do that; actually, you probably deserve to sit in on the interview," Martinez said. "But there's no way I can do that. It's procedure, and it wouldn't be safe if Thomas saw you. When

I'm done with the interview, the other deputies on the case and I will have a meeting to talk through everything we know—sort of like taking a bunch of puzzle pieces and seeing what we can get to fit together."

"Could you maybe call us?" Ashley asked.

"I could probably do that," Martinez said with a smile.

Ashley and Adam shook hands with Deputy Martinez, and another deputy led them out to the lobby. They got in the SUV, negotiated the myriad of one-way streets and traffic lights in downtown Colorado Springs, and headed north on Interstate 25.

Instead of going straight back to the campground, they exited the interstate and went west to the Garden of the Gods. The pristine red rock formations included the famed "Kissing Camels" rock, which really did look like two camels kissing.

Parking the SUV in the dirt, they sat on the rocks, which were still warm despite the overcast skies. Although the skies were still quite a few shades away from being blue, the afternoon was pleasant. Adam pulled a sweatshirt from the back of the vehicle while Ashley opened the back door on the driver's side and took out a blanket. They sat on a sloped red rock just off the road, next to the parked SUV.

"You realize this could be the end of the line, don't you?" Ashley asked Adam as he reclined on a rock. She was sitting, leaning back on her hands. "Adam, they have two of the guys. But those other two could be out of the state or even out of the country by now."

Adam closed his eyes for a second. He sat up and leaned onto his left arm to face his sister.

"I think they have two options," Adam said.

"Let's hear 'em," Ashley replied.

"One, they can try to sell the gold as it is. But with all the news coverage of the crime, someone could easily recognize it. I'd think that would make it hard for them to sell the gold for anywhere near its actual value."

"And the second option?" Ashley asked.

"They can try to extract the gold before they sell it," Adam said. "The crystals are probably worthless to them as they are now. They have to lug them around with them wherever they go."

"Good point," Ashley said. "This isn't something they can fit in their pocket. And remember, the tour guide at the Mollie-Kathleen said Thomas had asked for information about melting down gold."

"I don't think they've left Colorado," Adam said. "I wouldn't be surprised if these guys were cruising some seedy places in downtown Denver seeing if someone knew of a way to get rid of this gold. I mean, come on, Ash, these guys aren't Einsteins from what we know. It seems to me that Yarbrough was the brains behind the operation. But what I can't figure out is why they split up. Any thoughts on that one?"

"I think we can rule out greed," Ashley said. "If the two guys in the black 4Runner wanted to make all the money they could from the theft, they would have stuck with Yarbrough because he knew what was going on with separating the gold from the crystal—he was the chemist."

"So, you think there was a different reason?" Adam asked.

"Maybe they had a fight," Ashley said. "It could have involved Yarbrough and Thomas trying to slight the other two guys. Then maybe the other guys found out before they were supposed to or something like that."

"What you're saying, then, is that these guys who have the gold are on the run?" Adam asked.

"That's my best guess," Ashley said, standing up and brushing the red dirt from her jeans. "I think they're on the run and haven't a clue where to go. And since we keep catching them in the open, it doesn't seem like they have anywhere to hide."

"Nowhere to run, nowhere to hide," Adam said. "But how long can they survive like that?"

Ashley shrugged her shoulders as Adam picked up his sweatshirt and got into the car. They would have to hurry to make it back to the campground in time for dinner.

A Campout and a Breakout

It was Monday, and another overnight trip was planned for Thursday and Friday. The family would be in Sterling, less than two hours from where the chase of the 4Runner took place earlier in the week. But this would be a family trip. Mr. Arlington's former roommate from law school, Matt Foster, was the district attorney, and his office was in Sterling. The family would stay with the Fosters, and Ashley would get to visit Northeastern Junior College. She wasn't overly excited about going to a junior college, because her academic standing would qualify her for Ivy League schools. However, her goal was to play Division I basketball at a four-year college, so the junior college route might be an option if no Division I school offered a scholarship.

After hearing her children's report of the previous day's events, especially the part about the guns, Mrs. Arlington wasn't about to yield to their request to use the SUV on their own again.

"We're all going together, and we'll stay together," she said. Mr. Arlington nodded, and Ashley and Adam knew there would be no negotiation on this issue.

That night, Ashley and Adam walked down to a convenience store just outside the campground to get a soda. While they were there, Adam called Martinez on his pager. Martinez called back on the Arlingtons' cell phone minutes later, and Adam answered.

"How are you two doing?" Martinez asked.

"We've been officially taken out of the loop by our parents," Adam said.

"I had a feeling that was coming," Martinez said with a laugh.

"Deputy Martinez, we're leaving Thursday to go to Sterling for a couple of days," Adam said. "So, we just want to know if there's anything you can tell us about what happened with Thomas today?"

"I think we did all right with him," Martinez said. "We got the name of the fourth guy who's involved. He's Jack Johnson, another New Yorker with a record as long as Interstate 25. I don't know why Thomas gave us Johnson's name, unless Brookholder and Johnson are cutting out on Thomas and Yarbrough. But neither Brookholder nor Johnson seem like guys who would know what to do with the gold. I'm convinced that this is Yarbrough's scam since he has the smarts to extract the gold from the crystal. So once you helped us get him, the plan came apart at the seams. Now Brookholder and Johnson are just ad-libbing every step. They don't know what to do with those rocks except sit on them and stay out of sight.

"We didn't expect Thomas to cooperate, but we got more out of him than we thought we would. He said he barely knows Brookholder and Johnson. He won't implicate Yarbrough, but we didn't expect him to. Thomas made it sound like the two guys in the 4Runner just bolted the day the gold was stolen. He didn't admit to having the gold or even seeing it, but there's no question he knew the plan and was in line for some money. And I really think his story is believable.

"He wants to plead out, which means a plea bargain once charges are brought against him. We can hold him on the weapons charges and resisting arrest, so we won't have to return him to Limon to face the escape charge until we're done with him. We need to work some more information out of him.

"I'd guess this theft was Yarbrough's idea from start to finish, that he had the plans to cash in on the gold, but he couldn't do it alone. Thomas probably helped cover Johnson as Johnson took the gold—maybe Thomas even helped him out of the cave with it. We think Johnson hiked down the hill and put the gold straight in the 4Runner, and he and Brookholder, the driver, took off. Maybe Brookholder and Johnson decided they didn't want to wait for Yarbrough or Thomas, or maybe they figured the two wouldn't be able to get out of there once they saw the police. It sounds to me like they thought no one would notice that the gold was gone until the next day."

"So, even though all four men were in on the plan to steal the gold crystals, they had to split up two and two when the police showed up so suddenly and unexpectedly at Cave of the Winds?" Adam asked.

"The guys in the 4Runner probably thought they had no choice but to make a run for it," Martinez concluded. "I'd guess that all the police showing up killed their plan to rendezvous with Yarbrough and Thomas, and that being chased by the police confused the situation even more."

"I'll let Ashley know what's going on," Adam said.

"Good, and give both her and your parents my regards," Deputy Martinez said.

"Thanks. We'll talk again when my family gets back from Sterling," Adam said.

"Anytime," Martinez said. "See you."

Once off the phone, Adam filled Ashley in on what had happened.

"That's pretty much what we thought," Ashley said. "Although I have to admit, I'm still not sure why those guys are staying in Colorado. And if they're career criminals, why haven't they dumped the 4Runner?"

"Then they'd just have to steal another car, and the police would be looking for that," Adam said.

"Not necessarily," Ashley said. "They could spend a couple of hundred dollars and get an old clunker to get around in. And the police would have a hard time finding them in that case."

"Yeah, but they must think they need a four-wheel drive vehicle. I'm no car salesman, Ash, but I wouldn't think any working four-wheel drive vehicle would go for just a couple of hundred bucks," Adam said with a bit of sarcasm.

"Okay, maybe," Ashley said.

"We should probably get back to the campground," Adam said. "Mom and Dad are going to wonder why we've been gone so long."

They headed back to the campground and made sure they told their parents what was going on with the case.

"Sounds like it might be coming to an end," Mrs. Arlington said. "That's good news for everyone. I hope they find the gold."

With two open days before the trip to northeastern Colorado, the Arlingtons planned to do some sightseeing. There was so much to do in Colorado Springs that the family could have spent their entire vacation there and still not had enough time to see everything. But then Mr. and Mrs. Arlington began talking about what had happened in the case.

"Alex," Mrs. Arlington said. "I think we should head north now and find some activities up there."

"I agree," her husband said. "I don't think the kids are in any real danger here. But the farther we get them away from here, the less likely they are to be consumed by this case every minute of every day."

"So," she suggested, "let's head to the real woods."

"Real woods?" he asked.

"Yes. Let's take a tent and the sleeping bags and go to Rocky Mountain National Park," she said.

"There's an idea!" Mr. Arlington agreed.

"Camping is always fun," Adam said. "Plus, it's been cold and rainy for a couple of days. Now that it's nice, we might as well make the most of it."

"Yeah, it'll be nice being out in the wild," Ashley said. "We haven't slept in a tent together for a long time. It'll be kind of neat."

"Estes Park is beautiful this time of the year," Mrs. Arlington said. "We'll stop there and then stay two nights in Rocky Mountain National Park. It'll be fun."

The family loaded up the SUV with everything they would need for the two nights in Rocky Mountain National Park and the two days following that in northeastern Colorado.

They packed a pair of camping lanterns, two air mattresses and the tent, as well as four sleeping bags and the propane-powered stove. The Arlingtons would pick up supplies in the town of Estes Park, just outside the national park. Since they wouldn't be in Estes Park until about 3:00 P.M. the following day, they planned to get steak and chicken at a grocery store in town and cook out that night after hiking to the camping area. Dinner the next night would be heated beans and franks if their planned fishing venture failed.

"That sounds like a good plan," Mr. Arlington said. "We'll have plenty of water for oatmeal in the morning and more than enough canned food to heat for the afternoon meal. So, either we catch dinner the second night when we're fishing, or we just heat up something."

"If we go fish-less," Adam said, "we'll be ready for a big breakfast the second morning in the park before we leave for Sterling."

"I'll plan on that being the case," Mrs. Arlington said with a smile. "Of course, you never know, since Ashley and I are taking our poles. We'll probably bring home the bacon—or make that the fish fillets—for you boys."

Mr. Arlington smiled. "That sounds like a challenge," he said. "What do you say, Adam?"

"Girls against boys?" Adam said. "I don't know, Dad. How about Mom and I against you and Ashley?"

"Adam!" he said, smiling. "How about a vote for your old man?"

"Okay, okay," Adam said. "But let me know now, Mom. What are Dad and I going to lose in this bet?"

"The losers have to clean up the campground and pack the winners' backpacks before we hike back to the SUV the second morning," Mrs. Arlington said.

"And don't forget, guys," Ashley said. "I like my pack zipped all the way around, not one of those lazy-man zip jobs where the corners are opened and bugs can get into it."

"We'll see, Ash," Adam said, grinning.

The phone rang in the motor home. Their dad was closest to it and picked it up.

"Hello, Paul," he said. "How are you?"

"Fine, Alex," Martinez said. "I'm very sorry to bother you this late."

"That's all right, we're just planning a camping trip," he said.

"So, Adam and Ashley are home?" Martinez asked.

"Yes," Mr. Arlington answered. "Both of them. Which one would you like to speak with?"

"Actually, I'd just as soon talk to you," Martinez said.

"Okay," their father said. "I get the impression that something is up."

"More like something is out," Martinez said.

"Come again, Paul—I don't follow you," Mr. Arlington questioned.

"Alex," Martinez said, "you said you're headed off on a camping trip. Are you and the whole family headed out of town in the morning?"

"Bright and early," Mr. Arlington replied. "What's going on?"

"We had a bad situation at the jail," Martinez said. "Remember Kevin Yarbrough, the man who worked at Cave of the Winds, the one whose picture your daughter saw at the University of Colorado?"

"I've heard both Adam and Ashley use his name," Mr. Arlington said. "But no, I don't have any further recollection of him than that."

"We have nothing but bad recollections of him," Martinez said. "He escaped from jail tonight." Mr. Arlington asked Martinez to hold on for a moment. He covered the receiver with his hand and told Mrs. Arlington and the kids what had happened. Then he resumed his conversation with Martinez.

"We had Thomas out of his cell for questioning, and then we were going to bring Yarbrough in to tie up some loose ends. But he was able to get some sort of detergent from an inmate who was working in the laundry. Yarbrough had it in his mouth and spat it at the deputy who was bringing him down. He slipped out the door just about a half hour ago. A witness said she saw him get in a black sport utility vehicle just a few blocks away. If that's the case, we could have a hard time catching him."

"Did you say a black SUV?" Mr. Arlington asked. "Like the one I've heard so much about?"

"I'm afraid so," Martinez said. "We're thinking that's who Yarbrough called with his one phone call. It seemed like he might've had plans to have the guy, or guys, in the black SUV break him out of jail, although we don't know that for sure. In any event, it appears one of the two men still at large drove Yarbrough away."

"Interesting," Mr. Arlington said. "Well, should we do anything?"

"I don't think there's anything you can do," Martinez said. "I was just worried that Adam and Ashley would find out on the news late tonight or tomorrow and try to help with the search. I know neither you nor I want to see them put themselves in that kind of danger."

"Thank you," their dad said. "I think heading out of town tomorrow is probably the best for everyone involved."

"Well, maybe not for the criminals," Martinez said with a chuckle. "Your kids have had more luck tracking them down than we have. Anyway, have a good trip."

"We'll be gone for four days," Mr. Arlington said. "We'll call you when we get back in the Springs and check in with you to see if you have any new developments."

"Thanks for your help, Alex," Martinez said. "Good night."

Mr. and Mrs. Arlington knew the wheels in the kids' minds were spinning. They decided to call it a night a little early, since there was another full day of driving and hiking ahead.

Ashley and Adam talked in the front of the motor home after their parents had gone to bed in the back room.

"Where could the criminals go?" Adam asked.

"That's the big question," Ashley answered. "It does seem pretty obvious that Brookholder and Johnson ran out of ideas about what to do with the gold, where to go with it, or who to contact about getting rid of it."

"So, what you're saying," Adam figured, "is that Yarbrough is their key to the money?"

"Yep," Ashley said. "He's the brains behind the whole thing, just like we thought."

"I bet they knew Thomas would crack when the police caught him," Adam said. "And remember what Martinez said about Yarbrough? He said Yarbrough wasn't talking.

So Thomas probably wasn't in this too deeply, as far as knowing what Yarbrough's plans were for the gold. He was probably just in it for a big and easy payday."

"That would be my guess, too," Ashley said. "Oh well, let's get some sleep. We'll be out of the loop on this until early next week, if we ever get back in on it at all."

"It will probably be over by then," Adam said.

"You think the police will solve it or catch them all?" Ashley asked.

"No, I think once Yarbrough and those guys get the gold, they'll be out of Colorado, and probably out of the country before you can say 'New York, New York'," Adam said.

"That's probably right," Ashley said, smiling. "But we've got a lot of hiking in front of us, so we'd better call it a night."

"And you've got a campground to clean up in a couple of days," Adam said with a smile. "And be sure to put my dirty socks deep in the pack. I don't want them smelling everything else up."

Ashley grimaced.

"We'll see about that one," she said. "If I were a betting person, I'd take Mom and me."

Luck at the Lab and the Lake

The following morning wasn't as cold as the previous mornings had been. Instead of their traditional morning run, Mrs. Arlington guided the family through some interval training: sprinting for a while, jogging, more sprinting, and finally wrapping up with a ten-minute walk to cool down. The family stretched for several minutes before cleaning up and hitting the road.

After stopping for a drive-through breakfast just north of Colorado Springs, the family hit the outskirts of Denver as they headed north on Interstate 25. The long trek through the state capital city seemed to take a while.

"I'm glad I don't have to drive through this during rush hour every day," Mrs. Arlington said as she steered the

SUV to the right lane to let several vehicles pass on the left. "But, hey, look at the clock; we're still making good time. We'll be in the park before noon at this rate."

"Wait," Ashley said. "Could we stop in Boulder then, since we have some extra time? You and Dad could see the campus at the University of Colorado. It's not far out of the way, and we could pick up some more information at the registrar's office. We ran out of time when Adam and I visited last week. This could save us the hassle of having to call the university when we get back home."

"I have no problem with that," her mom said. Her dad and Adam also agreed to the side trip, which wasn't far out of the way.

"After we get done at CU, we'll just head up through Longmont and Lyons before we hit Loveland," her dad said, looking at the map. "We can pick up a few newspapers on the way and then stop in Estes Park before we get to the entrance of Rocky Mountain National Park."

"It's a plan," said Mrs. Arlington. As they rolled through Denver, she saw the sign for Boulder and exited. The family parked in front of the registrar's office, and everyone went inside with Ashley for admission papers.

"You guys want to walk to the chemistry building?" Ashley asked. "It's quite a setup out here."

"Sure," Mrs. Arlington said. "It'll stretch us out after all that hard running this morning. We'll get some of that lactic acid off our muscles so we'll be fresher for the hike at the park this afternoon."

They turned and headed down a sidewalk with a picture-perfect view of the mountains, which seemed to start right at the edge of the campus.

"Not many students or professors are around now," Mr. Arlington noted, looking around at the mostly empty parking lots.

"Summer school is going on," Ashley said, "but the department secretary in the chemistry building said it would be pretty desolate here until mid-August."

"Look at that car," her dad said, looking to his left, as the other three in the family looked toward the mountains to the right. "Couldn't be in a better parking place. And what luck; looks like it belongs to a tourist—New York plates."

Adam and Ashley spun around.

There in the parking lot, less than 20 feet away from them, was the black 4Runner with New York plates.

"Dad," Adam said. "Let's calmly walk to those trees over there. We need to make a phone call right away."

"What's going on, Adam?" asked Mrs. Arlington, who was confused. She turned around as Ashley guided her toward some small trees. Adam grabbed his dad's arm to do the same.

"Mom, that's the vehicle," Ashley said in a whisper as her parents leaned in to hear her. "Those are the guys who stole the gold, who we chased that day on the last overnight trip. We're going to go call 911."

"I'm going to go look in the car," Adam said, stopping suddenly. "I'll just peek in the windows. I won't open the doors or anything."

"Good intentions, bad plan," his father said, grabbing Adam's arm. "We'll call the police instead."

Mr. Arlington dialed 911. Ashley used the second cell phone to call Deputy Martinez. She was put on hold for what seemed like forever until she heard Deputy Martinez's familiar voice.

"Deputy Martinez, may I help you?" he said.

"This is Ashley Arlington, and I hope so," Ashley said.

"Hi, Ashley," Martinez said. "Don't tell me, let me guess: You and your brother caught the bad guys."

"No," Ashley said. "But we have found them, and my father is on the phone right next to me, calling 911. We're at the University of Colorado in Boulder. We can see the black 4Runner from where we're standing, and the plates match the ones we saw before."

"In Boulder?" Martinez said. "What could they be doing there?"

Ashley tapped her pen against her leg and then put the pieces together.

"My guess is that they're here to use some equipment or something in the chemistry lab," Ashley said. "Maybe they have a way of getting the gold into a more usable state, or maybe they're just analyzing it."

"Wow," Martinez said. "Good work."

"Now that I think about it," Ashley said, "we probably could have figured out that this would be one of the places they were likely to go. Yarbrough had been here for at least a couple of days when he interviewed, so he'd know the chem lab equipment and what it can do. And since it's summer, there's almost no one around here."

Mr. Arlington hung up.

"Come on, let's go," he said. "Ashley, move. We're supposed to get away from here as fast as we can."

"I'll talk to you later, Deputy Martinez," Ashley said quickly.

As flashing lights appeared around the corner, the Arlingtons walked quickly back toward the registrar's office. They went upstairs in the first building they came to and watched six police cars pull into the chemistry department parking lot. Two officers went through the 4Runner as eight went into the chemistry building. Not long after, two men were brought out in handcuffs.

"That first one is Brookholder," Adam said.

"The second one is Yarbrough," Ashley added. "He's the one who had hoped to teach here."

Just then, another police officer emerged with something shiny on what appeared to be a quilt or blanket.

"That's one of the gold crystals!" Ashley said, pointing excitedly.

"That's probably the smaller of the two pieces that were stolen," Adam said. "Unless another policeman comes out with a bigger piece, it's either still inside, in the 4Runner, or somewhere else."

"Good work, you two," their mother said, putting an arm around each of her kids. "Now, let's wait until the police car with those two criminals in it pulls out of the parking lot before we leave."

"Leave?" Ashley asked. "We have to find out what the police found—you know, find out what's going on."

"Nothing's going on right now as far as we're concerned, Ashley," her father said. "We've handled this the right way, and the police will take it from here. We don't know these police officers the way we know Paul Martinez. Even if we asked them what they've found, we'd only be in the way. We'll find out soon enough. Let's hit the road."

The Arlingtons watched as Brookholder and Yarbrough were driven away from the campus. The other officers emerged from the chem lab, but none of them carried the other gold crystal. At least three of the four men involved in the crime at the cave were in custody.

However, one more man and a big piece of gold were still out there somewhere.

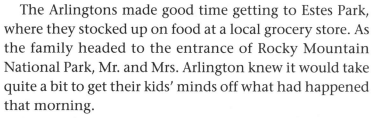

The Arlingtons made good time getting to Estes Park, where they stocked up on food at a local grocery store. As the family headed to the entrance of Rocky Mountain National Park, Mr. and Mrs. Arlington knew it would take quite a bit to get their kids' minds off what had happened that morning.

But Rocky Mountain National Park was more than "quite a bit"—it was downright breathtaking.

After they paid the entrance fee, the family parked well inside the park and got out of the SUV, loading up the backpacks and dividing the heavier things evenly for the trek into the woods. The four-person tent with fold-out poles was light, and was folded inside a small bag that fit comfortably below the sleeping bag on Mr. Arlington's backpack.

At the entrance they had received a map and tips on the best places to camp, as well as areas to avoid so they wouldn't disturb the wildlife. The Arlingtons set out at 2:45 P.M., and after about an hour and a half of walking uphill at a decent pace, they found a clearing surrounded by trees. At that elevation, it was cold. After setting up the tent and getting everything organized, everyone changed into pants and sweatshirts or jackets.

Adam and his mother went north to explore while Ashley and her father went south. They agreed to meet back at the camp in thirty minutes. It was only a brief trip, but the Arlingtons were careful to put safety first in an area where beauty belied the inherent danger of the surroundings.

"Take it as slowly as you think you need to and then take it even slower," Mrs. Arlington said. "Let's have a little fun without anyone getting hurt."

Adam and his mother found a heavily wooded area that had some branches lying around. They gathered quite a few and headed back after hiking for only about fifteen minutes. Ashley and her father found a lake and a stream for fishing just over a hill from the camp.

"This will be perfect," Ashley said.

"Great," Mr. Arlington said with a smile. "Having both the stream and the lake should give Adam and me enough fish to keep us busy for the day."

"We'll see about that," Ashley said. "How long have we been out here, about twenty minutes?"

"About that," he said, looking at his watch. "We should head back now."

The two pairs exchanged information when they returned. Adam and Ashley carefully started a cooking fire as Mr. Arlington pulled out the tightly wrapped chicken and steak they had bought at the grocery store in town. As the family ate, darkness came, but not before the Arlingtons were able to take in another picturesque sunset.

But with the departing sun came even colder temperatures. Rather than stay outside, the family retreated into the tent, which at first was equally cold. But once Mrs. Arlington turned on a propane lamp, the tent warmed up quickly.

"I can't believe I left my computer down in the car," Adam said as everyone else pulled out a book to read.

"That thing, to you, has almost been like Ashley's teddy bear was to her," said their mom with a smile.

"Hey, I do a lot of reading on my computer," Adam said. "I hardly ever play games on it anymore."

"I know," Mrs. Arlington said. Still, Adam was the only one without a book, so no one else felt right reading quietly and leaving him on his own. They decided to choose one book to read out loud.

"If you want, Adam," said Mr. Arlington, "we can read your mother's romance novel, or Ashley's book, which is . . . what is it?"

Ashley held up the cover of her biography for her parents and brother to see.

Mr. Arlington read them the entire first chapter of Ashley's book. As he prepared to read the second chapter, his wife tapped him on the arm. Ashley and Adam were asleep.

"I didn't even notice," he said. "When did they go out?"

"Well, I think Adam lasted until about three or four pages ago," she whispered, "but I think Ashley was out when you opened the cover."

Knowing they were at such a high altitude, the Arlingtons did without a run the following morning. Instead, Mr. Arlington led the family on a brisk walk, stopping several times to discuss the things they saw. After a breakfast of oatmeal made with water warmed on the fire, the family set out for their fishing derby.

Adam caught a fish with his first cast, and it appeared his mom and Ashley were in for a long wait that day and a busy morning of cleaning camp the next.

"That's a big rainbow trout," his dad said, looking at Adam's catch as he pulled it out of the water. "That'll just about feed us tonight."

The fish was indeed impressive and would make a good meal. But Adam's fishing luck took a dive, and his father never had any. Mrs. Arlington pulled in the next two fish, and Ashley pulled in four more after that. The family kept only two, releasing the other fish safely into the lake. Since they had more luck fishing than they had planned—or at least Ashley and Mrs. Arlington did—the family decided to have a big, late lunch instead of waiting for dinner.

Adam and Ashley took care of cleaning one fish apiece while Mr. Arlington prepared to do the cooking.

"This is the life," Adam said. "Great food, great surroundings, and great company."

"And a great big mess that I'll have nothing to do with tomorrow," Ashley said with a smile.

"Let's try and keep it a little clean," Mr. Arlington said, playfully flipping Ashley's napkin back toward her after she dropped it.

Later the Arlingtons played Frisbee, but they returned to the campsite before dark.

"I've got a surprise," Mrs. Arlington said, opening her backpack. "Marshmallows!"

"Good job, Mom!" Adam said.

"I'll have a handful," Ashley added.

Everyone scurried around the campsite to find a stick suitable for roasting marshmallows over the open fire. Adam found the best stick, piling two marshmallows onto the tip and one onto each of the three separate branches on the stick's sides.

"Showoff," Ashley said, pushing his stick out of the way with hers, which wasn't as practical but was much thicker.

"You can have one of these," Adam said with a smile. "And I guarantee you it will be perfect."

The marshmallows didn't last long. With the exception of the two Adam dropped into the fire in his quest for the perfect marshmallow, the Arlingtons finished off the bag in a hurry.

As the wind picked up, the temperature dropped. Since the first can of propane had burned out just after Mr. Arlington had put down the book the night before, he went to his backpack and got another container. After cranking the lamp up to its highest setting, the family got into their warm sleeping bags and huddled around the heat of the lamp. Mr. Arlington picked up Ashley's book.

Adam filled his sister in on chapter one of the book, then their father started reading chapter two aloud. He read for another half hour. This time, it was Adam who went out in a hurry.

"He must have dozed off thinking about all the ones that got away today," Ashley whispered to her parents as she broke into a wide grin.

"We'll call it a night early," Mrs. Arlington whispered to her husband, "because you boys have some cleaning and packing to do in the morning."

A bet is a bet, but Ashley and her mother couldn't bear to watch Mr. Arlington and Adam do all the work the next morning. They pitched in by making a breakfast of oatmeal and fruit.

The hike back to the SUV took a lot of focus and attention. Although hiking downhill was easier than hiking uphill, Mrs. Arlington cautioned about how one misstep heading down a hill could put someone on crutches quite easily.

After loading up the SUV, the family headed out of the park. A beautiful drive down Big Thompson Canyon took the Arlingtons to Interstate 25. They soon exited, heading east on State Highway 14. Adam sighed as they approached the turn to Ault, the memory of nearly catching the 4Runner still etched in the back of his mind.

Mr. Arlington slowed and turned into Ault, and Adam and Ashley showed him the intersection where the 4Runner had just beat an oncoming train. The family decided to eat at a diner in Ault, and as the Arlingtons ate, two trains passed through the same intersection. The family piled back into the vehicle and soon arrived in Sterling at the Fosters' house.

Mr. Arlington's old friend Matt Foster had changed little. He and his wife had twin girls, both of whom were in high school. They took Adam to the mall the next day while Ashley visited Northeastern Junior College. She was impressed with the coach and the school, but could not stop thinking about the University of Colorado in Boulder.

Mrs. Arlington called their motor home that evening to check the family's voice mail messages. The first one was from Deputy Martinez.

"Hi, it's Deputy Martinez," the message said. "I figured you wouldn't be back yet, but I thought I'd let you know that we do have three of the men in custody, as well as the smaller of the two pieces of gold crystals. We have had two possible sightings of Jack Johnson, and we're following up on those now. Anyway, good work. I just wanted to keep you up-to-date. Oh, by the way, there is a reward, and I know the kids said they couldn't accept it. However, the money is yours to do with as you wish. Thanks, call if you want when you get back, and I hope you had a safe trip. Good-bye."

Mrs. Arlington pressed the button on the phone to play the second message.

"Hello, it's Paul Martinez again," the message said. "We're closing in on Johnson. He's trapped, and he knows it. Anyway, call when you get back. We don't have him yet, but we will soon."

Mrs. Arlington told Mr. Arlington and the kids about the messages. In turn, the Fosters wanted to know all about the case. Adam and Ashley filled them in on the story.

"That's some kind of summer vacation," Mr. Foster said. "Sounds like there hasn't been a dull moment."

Little did anyone know that the most exciting moment was yet to come.

The Last Man Out

There were only three days left in their vacation when the family got back to Colorado Springs. They stopped and picked up a pizza on the way back to the motor home. Mrs. Arlington remembered that she had packed several of the family's favorite movies. It was nice to put a movie in the VCR as they all wound down while eating the pizza.

It was a little past 9:00 P.M. when the movie ended. Mr. Arlington picked up the pizza box, and Ashley took care of the soda cans and napkins. The family then divided up the tasks that had to be done in the short time frame. Adam would do two loads of laundry the following morning. He would also go over the route home on his computer atlas and reconfirm the travel plans, marking likely stopping places and possible tourist attractions or historical areas the family could visit.

Ashley and her dad would handle the cleaning of the motor home, emptying the sewage and taking out all the trash. Her parents would remount the SUV onto the car carrier, but not until the night before the family was to leave. Mrs. Arlington would be in charge of checking out from the campground.

After everyone had written down their responsibilities, the phone rang. Everyone assumed it was Deputy Martinez, and they were right. Mrs. Arlington was the closest, so she answered.

"Hello," she said. "How are you doing?"

"Good," Deputy Martinez said. "I hope your trip was both safe and fun."

"It was both," she said. "And thanks for the messages."

"So, you got both of them?" Martinez asked.

"Yes, we did," she replied. "It sounds like that's some good news for you all."

"It sure is," Martinez said. "And a lot of this, most of it, came about because of your kids' help."

"I'll pass that along," she said. "We always tell them that they should help the police whenever possible. Because Alex is a lawyer, we know what all of you in law enforcement are up against these days."

"We appreciate that," Martinez said, "and I think I have a way to thank Adam and Ashley. We've located Jack Johnson, the final person missing from this manhunt, through a lead on a stolen car. We tailed him to a motel downtown," Martinez said. "We searched the car, but no gold. When he went to eat after checking into the motel, we checked his room. But we found nothing there, either."

"That's too bad," Mrs. Arlington said. "What's your next step?"

"We're going to give this guy one more chance, tomorrow morning," Martinez said. "We'll see where he goes and whether he leads us to the gold. Then we'll arrest him."

"Let us know how it goes, if you don't mind," she said. "We're leaving in a few days, and I know both Ashley and Adam would like to hear how this turns out."

"Hear how it turns out?" Martinez repeated. "If it is all right with you and Alex, we want Ashley and Adam to *see* how it turns out."

Their mom was puzzled and asked for clarification. "Obviously, my kids wouldn't be in harm's way at all," she said questioningly.

"No, of course not," Martinez said. "We sometimes take observers on ride-alongs. Tomorrow I'd like to take Adam and Ashley, if it's all right with you and Alex. We'll be in a safe car far back in the line of defense. We'll be close enough to see what's going on but far enough away that, even in a worst case scenario, they wouldn't be in any danger."

"I understand," Mrs. Arlington said. "I'll talk to Alex and the kids and call you back within the hour."

She pulled her husband outside the motor home and told him about Paul Martinez's offer.

"I don't know, Anne," he said. "We've been preaching to the kids about the need to keep at a distance."

"That was my first thought, too," she said. "I was worried that they'd be so excited to be there that they wouldn't realize the danger. But as I thought about it more, I realized it would probably have just the opposite effect on them as the one you and I are worried about."

"Okay, you've got my attention," he said. "Let's hear it."

"Alex, I think that by actually being there Ashley and Adam will see how important it really is to stay back and let the police do their work," she said. "They'll see the police in action, and they'll also see that it's no place for them. Even being at a safe distance, they'll still get that sense of danger. Maybe they'll understand why police work is best left to the professionals, and both kids will get a sense of the risk and sacrifice involved in police work."

"I'm sold," her husband said. "You want to tell them, or should I?"

"I'll handle it," she replied, stepping up the stairs back into the motor home as he followed.

Mrs. Arlington sat Ashley and Adam down and explained the situation to them, telling them everything Martinez had told her, and then relaying both her own and their father's feelings.

"What your father and I are saying," she said, "is that it is okay with us, but the decision is yours."

Ashley and Adam looked at each other.

"It sounds safe, and I'd love to do it," Ashley said.

"I'm in, too," Adam said.

Ashley called Deputy Martinez and let him know that both she and Adam were ready to go whenever the police were, just as long as it happened before the family went home to Washington, D.C.

"How about tomorrow morning?" Martinez asked. "I'll come get you two at 6:00 A.M."

"We'll see you then," Ashley said. "Thanks for thinking about us and inviting us along."

"Hey, the thanking goes from us to you and your brother," Deputy Martinez said. "It really only seems fitting that you two are involved. Both your parents and I thought it would be best to keep your names under wraps. Meanwhile, I'm looking like Supercop because of your work and attention. So, this is a small way to pay you back. I'd like to take your family to lunch the day after tomorrow if that works, too. It's about time your dad and I caught up on old times now that this case is nearly wrapped up. And my wife and little girl would like to meet you."

Ashley asked her mother and father, who said that was fine. Besides, they would be leaving Colorado the day after, and all the cooking tools would be put away in the motor home.

"We can do that," Ashley said. "So, Adam and I will see you tomorrow morning for the ride-along, and then the next day the entire family will see you for lunch, right?"

"Right on the money," Martinez said. "Now get some sleep."

"Got it," Ashley said. "Good-bye."

Adam and Ashley went right to bed, knowing the next day would start early. When they woke up, they made sure they were ready fifteen minutes before Martinez was to pick them up. They didn't want to make him wait under any circumstances.

"Let's go, Adam. Don't use all the hot water," Ashley said, tapping on the door of the motor home's bathroom.

"Got ya," Adam said. "I'll be done in just a minute."

The two were ready in plenty of time and sat outside eating cereal and drinking juice under the motor home's awning.

"You know, I miss home, but I'll miss the beauty of this state," Ashley said, pointing toward the mountains, with

Pikes Peak standing out at the highest point. Trees dotted Colorado's front range of mountains with two small exceptions where strip mining had left a pair of decades-old red stone "scars."

"We have to come back here," Adam said. "I want to head toward the Utah border again north of Grand Junction to Dinosaur National Monument. And even though I liked CU, I'd still like to see the campus at Colorado State University in Fort Collins. They have some good computer programs. Oh well, I still have two years of high school left, so I have plenty of time to check it out."

"If I do end up in Boulder at CU," Ashley said, "you can come out here with me on a recruiting trip or when I move out here, and then you can take off for the day—but no chasing bad guys!"

They both laughed. After finishing their breakfast, they brushed their teeth and sat in the front of the motor home, catching a few news headlines on their big TV. Their parents were watching the same thing on a smaller TV in the back bedroom of the motor home.

Deputy Martinez pulled into the campground in an unmarked gray sedan. It still looked very much like a police car, with a searchlight above the mirror on the driver's side door and the blue and red lights perched in the back window.

"I'll sit up front," Adam said, "if that's okay with you two."

Ashley and Deputy Martinez agreed. They pulled out and headed downtown to the motel where Jack Johnson was staying. Ashley and Adam had seen many beautiful, well-kept motels and hotels through the course of their time in Colorado Springs.

The motel where Johnson was holed up was not one of those motels. In fact, it was run down quite badly.

Adam looked into the backseat toward Ashley. "Our motor home looks like the Hilton compared to this place," he quipped.

Ashley unlatched her seat belt and scooted to the middle of the backseat, leaning against the front seat for a better view of the motel.

"That's his room there—number seven," Martinez said.

They sat for about fifteen minutes, and nothing happened. Martinez started filling Adam and Ashley in on what had come of the bust at CU.

"It couldn't have unfolded any better for the law enforcement units that showed up there after your 911 call," Martinez said. "No one was hurt, and nothing was broken at the university. One of the campus parking interns had written down the number of the license plate about ten minutes before you got there. They were already running the plate at the campus police headquarters when you called 911. So campus police, city police, and the county sheriff were all there fewer than five minutes after you called. That's about as good as it gets."

"What else did they find on Brookholder and Yarbrough?" Ashley asked. "And what were they doing there?"

"They had just the smaller piece of gold crystal, so we think they were going to run some tests on it to see how much actual gold it contained. Maybe they wanted to get a box with the CU logo on it, so they could mail it to themselves out of the country or something like that," Martinez said. "We believe Johnson has the other, bigger piece somewhere. Brookholder and Yarbrough didn't really have anything else on them. Johnson may have been with Brookholder and Yarbrough near the time of their arrest; the car he stole was from up in that area. We're guessing he figured his pals had been busted, and he had to steal a car to get out of there. But we're still stunned that he came back to Colorado Springs. That's the last place I would have expected him to go after his three accomplices got busted."

"Maybe he just likes the food better in Limon State Prison," Ashley said with a grin.

"Maybe so," Martinez said. "But this guy is from New York, and if he'd have made tracks back there, I don't know if we'd have ever found him. I thought he would definitely head for New York or try to leave the country. He's a pretty tough guy, and I think he could've made it if he didn't do anything stupid."

Just then, Johnson came out of his room. There were four police cars and a van in the area, as well as a police helicopter a few miles away.

Johnson got into a small, blue sedan and headed toward Interstate 25. The police followed, and Ashley and Adam could hear on the police radio that other police units, in addition to the helicopter, were monitoring Johnson's progress as he headed north on I-25.

Johnson did not speed, exiting onto U.S. Highway 24 in the same manner as any other car.

"Excuse me, am I missing something?" Adam asked. "Are we headed to Cave of the Winds?"

Ashley and Adam looked at each other in shock. Was this guy really going back to the scene of the crime? And if he was, why?

"I think you're right," Martinez said, picking up his walkie-talkie.

"All units, this is Martinez," he said. "Be advised this is the exit that leads to Cave of the Winds, the site of the crime. The suspect does know this area; this is where he eluded police the first day."

Various units acknowledged, and the dispatcher gave the helicopter clearance to head in that direction. Johnson kept driving west toward the mountains and Cave of the Winds, slowing down and pulling to the side of the road at the bridge that lay less than a mile from the entrance road to the cave.

"Is he having car trouble? Can anyone tell what he's doing?" a police officer asked over the radio.

"This is where I saw them the day of the theft!" Ashley said.

"Negative," Martinez answered the officer into the radio. "This is where the suspects made their getaway that first day. But he doesn't have four-wheel drive this time, and he'll find the going rough. Let's just sit back and see what he's trying to do. There's only one house in the area, and that's quite a way from here. Still, we need to send a unit up to the house to make sure that if anyone is home, they are safe and aware of the situation."

A voice answered back that he would take care of that "right away." By that time, Johnson was struggling to navigate his small car over the bumpy terrain. The cloud of dust kicked up by the vehicle made him easy to track. Just then, Johnson's car slid sideways to a halt.

"Did he wipe out?" Martinez asked.

"No," Adam said. "Ashley, isn't that where you saw them spin out and stop that first day?"

"That's exactly the place; I remember the two trees next to the road there," Ashley said. "They stopped there, and when the dust blew down for a second, I was able to see their license plate."

Just then, Johnson got out of his car and walked behind one of the trees.

"Does he know we're following him?" Adam wondered.

"No, look!" Ashley said excitedly, pointing. "That green canvas bag he's picking up—they must have thrown it out when they stopped that day. They would have known something had gone wrong when the director of the Cave of the Winds came yelling about how the gold crystals had been stolen."

"So they ditched the big piece of gold crystal in case they got caught," Adam said. "They could've thrown the smaller piece out on the road anytime if they thought the police had them. But that wouldn't have ruined the plan, because they could have still come back here and gotten the big piece."

"This explains why they all stayed in Colorado," Martinez said. "They couldn't head out of state without the gold, but they knew they couldn't draw too much attention to themselves and come back here to get the bigger piece, at least not until the authorities had backed off a little bit and most of the attention the crime was getting had died down. A couple of days ago when they went to Boulder to the CU chem lab, I'll bet you they were going to figure out exactly what they had, head down here to pick up the big piece, and then not stop until they reached Mexico or Canada. Even with all of their mistakes and the fact that we had two of them behind bars pretty quickly, they still came within a day or so of pulling this thing off."

Johnson appeared to be unzipping the canvas bag. After looking inside, he picked it up and slung it over his shoulder. But as he hurried back toward his car, the bottom of the bag, moist from being left out during several days of rain, ripped.

Out came the gold crystal.

"There it is!" Adam said. "We've got him and the gold!"

Adam and Ashley could feel their hearts racing and their mouths going dry. The radio chirped as instructions were barked out.

"Copter one, move in above the crime scene," a voice said. "Unit Four, go in."

Unit Four was a four-wheel drive Expedition, larger than the Arlingtons' SUV and the only four-wheel drive vehicle among the police cars in the chase. As Unit Four put on its sirens and red lights, Johnson tried to pick up the gold crystal. In his agitation it slipped through his hands, and he let it go. He ran toward his car, hurled himself inside, and sped up the hill.

"He's got nowhere to go, nowhere to hide," Martinez said.

Almost as though he had heard Martinez, Johnson stopped, threw his car hard into reverse, and turned around, speeding toward the police vehicle. Realizing he had no chance to ram the bigger police Expedition, Johnson tried to turn around. But without four-wheel drive, his car went sailing, flipping over. The car came to a rest on its roof. As Johnson pulled himself out of the broken passenger-side window, police from Unit Four handcuffed him. The helicopter whirred overhead while several other officers on foot arrived at Johnson's car. One had a German shepherd from the canine unit.

Within a short time, a second wave of police descended on the scene. They were soon followed by a news van.

"Well," Martinez said, "it looks like we'll get some coverage on the news this evening. You know, I'm glad. I know it must sound a little silly to you two, but the police get so much negative coverage these days. I know some of it is deserved, but we also do a lot of good things that aren't always reported."

"You don't need to sell us," Ashley said. "We've seen your job up close the past few days. We have more respect for the police than ever before!"

"Sounds like you two learned a lot during this case," Martinez said.

Adam nodded his head.

"You betcha," he said.

"Like what?" Martinez asked.

"These criminals need driving lessons," Adam said. All three in the car laughed.

"That's true," Ashley said, still laughing. "Two of the four flipped their cars like they were pancakes."

The police at the scene recovered the gold crystal and wrapped it in a big, wool blanket.

"Someone will be happy to get that back," Adam said. He and Ashley looked at each other and smiled.

Closing the Case

The Arlingtons worked late into the night to get everything ready for their pending departure. Everyone felt a sense of relief that all four thieves had been caught and the gold crystals were now safe.

The next morning the entire family went to visit Cave of the Winds a final time. Driving down I-25 and exiting on U.S. Highway 24, Adam and Ashley showed their parents how the chase had unfolded the day before.

"Sounds like an exciting ending," Mrs. Arlington said.

"It was," Ashley answered. "But once Johnson left the highway here, it was basically all over."

"What surprises me," her dad said, "is that they would leave the gold crystal out here in the open. I can't believe it."

"I couldn't believe it either," Adam said. "But once the director discovered the crystals were missing, I think it threw the criminals' whole plan off."

The Arlingtons turned right and headed up the winding road to the cave. Adam and Ashley showed their parents where the gold crystals had been when they were stolen. The pieces of gold crystal would be in the police evidence room for a while, but Ashley and Adam knew the pieces would eventually be restored to their place in the cave. The Arlington teens both felt proud that they had helped make that possible.

The family waited in the lobby outside the cave entrance for Deputy Martinez and his family. He gave Alex a bear hug and introduced the Arlingtons to his wife, Christine, and his daughter, Tina.

"Shall we get some lunch?" Martinez asked.

After heading down the hill a couple of miles, the two vehicles pulled into the parking lot of a restaurant. They went inside and were seated at a large table. After everyone ordered, Martinez relayed what he had learned about the case's conclusion.

"We think we'll get plea bargains out of all of them," he said. "They are all afraid—each one thinks that the others will testify against him. We found out a little more about Yarbrough. He became a gambling addict in Cripple Creek and used up all the money he had earned overseas and the money he had gotten from his pyramid scheme. Adam's and Ashley's theory about how the plan went awry at the cave was correct. The missing gold crystals were discovered more quickly than the thieves had expected. They didn't know what to do when Jim figured it out so soon.

"All along, their plan was for Johnson to hike down the hill from the cave with the gold in the canvas bag, rather than have Yarbrough risk carrying the bag out from the gift shop, which might have aroused suspicion. But luckily Jim figured out the gold crystals were missing pretty quickly after it happened. Otherwise, Johnson would have already made it down the hill and we would never have seen the 4Runner driving away.

"They all managed to get away from Cave of the Winds the day of the heist, but that was the last bit of good luck they had. Their 'friendship' was strained when Yarbrough and Thomas asked afterward what had happened to the big piece of gold crystal. Johnson and Brookholder didn't tell Yarbrough that they had dumped it by the tree before they even got to Highway 24. They made up a story about how it had been stolen out of the 4Runner when they stopped for gas, and they told him all they had left was the smaller piece. So, Yarbrough took the smaller one to CU to measure it and weigh it, and to figure out how much the smaller piece was worth.

"Johnson and Brookholder were already conniving together behind the others' backs. They were going to let Yarbrough figure out how much the smaller piece was worth and then use that information to estimate how much the bigger piece was worth. They would get their cut of the smaller piece once Yarbrough sold it. After that, Brookholder and Johnson would sell the bigger piece without telling their other two 'partners,' Yarbrough or Thomas. Then they would only have to split the money two ways instead of four. That's why they only broke Yarbrough out of jail—they needed his expertise. But they kept getting tripped up along the way. They had no idea who kept catching up with them. Had it not been for Adam and Ashley, we might not have caught them."

The Arlingtons smiled and thanked Deputy Martinez for his kind words.

"Oh, and another thing," Martinez said, reaching into his back pocket for an envelope. "Jim Dockery from Cave of the Winds had posted a $1,000 reward. I didn't tell him who cracked the case, only that they wanted to remain anonymous. And that's fine; in fact, it's my department's policy. And here's another check from Crimestoppers, also for $1,000. You can also remain anonymous for that one."

Martinez set the two checks on the table. Aside from glancing at the checks, no one in the Arlington family picked them up.

"Crime only pays if you're preventing it," Adam said, causing everyone to laugh.

Mr. and Mrs. Arlington looked at their two children. Without saying a word, Adam and Ashley knew the right thing to do.

"Deputy Martinez," Ashley said. "We're very grateful that our efforts are appreciated. But we think accepting money for simply doing the right thing would be wrong. Could you donate this to your department's victim assistance fund? We have one of those back home. You do have one here too, right?"

"We sure do," Martinez said. "That's a really nice gesture. This money will make someone's day."

"It made our day too," Ashley said. "We just don't want to take it with us. This way, it will make our day again, knowing we helped someone else."

"You kids have already been paid too in another way by helping Deputy Martinez solve this case," Mrs. Arlington said. "Do you want to let him in on the important lessons you've learned, the ones you were telling us last night in the motor home?"

Ashley and Adam looked at each other. "Sure," they agreed.

"I'll go first," Adam said. "Now that I've had time to think about it, it's pretty obvious that the police, not the public, are the ones who are trained to solve crimes and who have the authority to chase and capture criminals. If a criminal has the audacity to commit a crime, then what's to keep him from pointing a gun at someone who is trying to interfere or chase him and pulling the trigger?"

"I like what Adam said, and I couldn't agree more," Ashley added. "There were times when I wanted to keep going and do more to catch these guys, but thinking about it now, we should have actually bowed out a lot sooner in most of the scenarios. It's far too dangerous work for untrained observers."

"I really did have fun, feeling like we had a part in catching three criminals who were wanted for committing a really bad crime," Adam said. "But it's just as important to give the police space to do their job. We were way too close to the chase in Alamosa. Like Deputy Martinez said, anytime the public can help out, the police welcome it. But there's a fine line that the public can't, and shouldn't, cross when it comes to that kind of thing. And I now know where that line is."

"That's a good observation, Adam," Mr. Arlington commented. "As an attorney, I see police cases that are actually hindered by untrained people getting too involved. It's important to be a good citizen and report crime to the police, but being a good citizen also involves letting the police take it from there and do their job."

"And I couldn't agree more with that," Deputy Martinez said with a smile. "As helpful as you kids were, even catching the criminals and recovering the stolen gold crystals could never be as important to my officers as your safety!"

Now it was Ashley's turn. "I guess the other thing I learned was how important it is to pay attention to details," she said. "We helped the police by paying attention to what seemed like little things. Solving the 'KY' initial puzzle came about just because we took good notes in the Cave of the Winds parking lot after the crime. We noticed a lot of little things about the cars everyone drove, and those things ended up being important details. The more you pay attention, the less you overlook."

"So how will you apply your lessons to life back in D.C. when we get home?" Mrs. Arlington asked.

"I know I'm going to take more notes—writing things down—instead of just taking 'mental' notes when I'm in classes or during basketball practice, or even just when I'm out with my friends. Having notes written down means I can come back to them later when I need information rather than trying to remember details all in my head."

"Good thinking, Ash," said Mr. Arlington. "How about you, Adam?"

"Well, I did learn one other lesson that I'm going to pay attention to back home," Adam said, even though he was a little embarrassed to bring it up in front of Deputy Martinez. "I never really thought of speeding as a big deal, but after chasing the 4Runner to Ault and seeing both Thomas and Johnson flip their cars over, I realize more than ever that speed limits are set for a good reason. Thomas's car flipped near a residential area—he could have killed a pedestrian, another innocent driver, or himself. Speeding isn't worth the price you could pay for it—not just a ticket, but maybe someone's life!"

"I'm glad you realize that," Deputy Martinez said seriously. "You didn't mention anything before about chasing that 4Runner, just that you spotted it. I'm sorry to hear that you risked that. But at least I think you've learned a valuable lesson—one I hope you won't forget!"

"I won't, sir," promised Adam, "and I'm going to tell my friends about it, too. They haven't always followed the speed limit either, but we will when I'm in the group from now on if I have anything to say about it."

"Good for you!" everyone agreed.

"I'm pretty proud of you two for your efforts, and for thinking so carefully about what you have learned," Mrs. Arlington said.

"These are a couple of special kids you've got here, Alex and Anne," Paul Martinez said again. The Arlingtons smiled.

"Thanks for everything you've done, Paul, and for what you've helped teach our kids this summer," Mr. Arlington responded. He and Deputy Martinez spent the rest of the time talking about their days together as buddies in the Army Reserves, making both families laugh at the funny incidents they remembered.

Ashley and Adam also had fun getting to know Tina Martinez. She was much younger than the Arlington kids, but she already shared their excitement about her dad's line of work. Someday, she said, she wanted to be a "deputy just like Daddy."

When they had finished their lunches, both families got ready to leave. Everyone stood and headed toward the door. Out in the parking lot, they shook hands and said good-bye.

"We'll be leaving bright and early in the morning," Mrs. Arlington said. "We're going to head out a day early. That way we won't have to rush the trip home as much."

"You all deserve a *real* vacation after this," Martinez said, smiling.

The two families exchanged a final wave before they turned separate ways leaving the restaurant's parking lot.

"Kind of hard to believe it's all over," Adam said to Ashley. "We won't forget this vacation."

"No kidding," Ashley said. "Maybe on the trip home, we could find some caves to visit."

"Oh no! Everybody duck! Here come the bats!" Adam yelled from the backseat.

Everyone laughed as Mr. Arlington steered the SUV down the highway and back to the campground.

Colorado

Fun
Fact
Files

Colorado

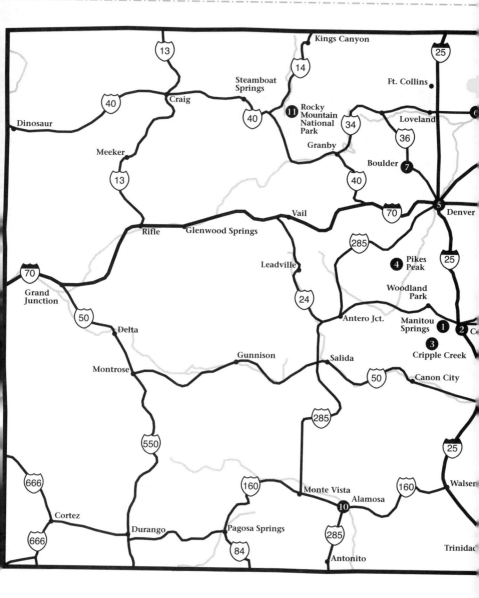

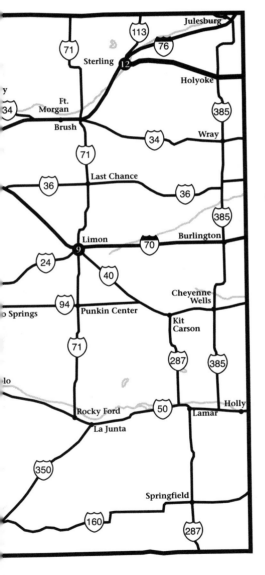

The Arlingtons' Route

1. Manitou Springs
2. Colorado Springs
3. Cripple Creek
4. Pikes Peak
5. Denver
6. Greeley
7. Boulder
8. Ault
9. Limon
10. Alamosa
11. Rocky Mountain National Park
12. Sterling

Names and Symbols

Origin of Name:

Colorado is from the Spanish, meaning "ruddy" or "red."

Nickname:

Centennial State

Motto:

Nil sine Numine—"Nothing without Providence"

State Symbols:

flower—Rocky Mountain columbine
tree—Colorado blue spruce
bird—lark bunting
animal—Rocky Mountain bighorn sheep
gemstone—aquamarine
colors—blue and white
song—"Where the Columbines Grow"
fossil—stegosaurus

Geography

Location:

West-central United States; one of the Rocky Mountain states

Borders:

Wyoming (north)
Nebraska (north and east)
Kansas (east)
Oklahoma (southeast)
New Mexico (south)
Arizona (southwest)
Utah (west)

Area:

104,247 square miles (8th largest state)

Highest elevation:

Mt. Elbert (14,433 feet)

Lowest elevation:

Arkansas River (3,350 feet)

Nature

National Parks:

Rocky Mountain
Mesa Verde

National Forests:

Arapaho National Forest
Grand Mesa National Forest
Gunnison National Forest
Medicine Bow-Routt National Forest
Pike National Forest
Rio Grande National Forest
Roosevelt National Forest
San Isabel National Forest
San Juan National Forest
Uncompahgre National Forest
White River National Forest

Weather:

Colorado is generally sunny and dry, although weather conditions can vary greatly in differences of altitude—for instance, cool summers and snowy winters are typical of the more mountainous areas. The highest recorded temperature is 118 degrees, while the lowest recorded temperature is 61 degrees below zero.

People and Cities

Population:

3,970,971 (1998 census)

Capital:

Denver

Ten Largest Cities (as of 1998):

Denver (499,055)

Colorado Springs (344,987)
Aurora (250,604)
Lakewood (136,883)
Fort Collins (108,905)
Pueblo (107,301)
Arvada (97,610)
Westminster (95,691)
Boulder (90,543)
Thornton (74,139)

Counties:

63

Major Industries

Agriculture:

Agriculture is still an important part of Colorado's economy. The primary product is cattle. Other important crops are corn, hay, wheat, milk, and sugar beets.

Mining:

Times are changing! Mining was once very important to Colorado's economy, especially with the discovery of gold, silver, and lead. Although Denver is home to companies that control half the nation's gold production, the mining industry now employs only 1.2 percent of Colorado's state workforce. However, the industry continues with the mining of molybdenum, sand and gravel, uranium, coal, and petroleum.

Manufacturing:

Since the 1950s, manufacturing has been the biggest money-maker for Colorado. The most important products are food and related items, and printing and publishing. Colorado also manufactures primary metals, instruments, and stone, clay, and glass products.

Tourism:

Six billion dollars are spent each year in the tourism industry, 1.8 billion of that being spent on Colorado's ski slopes, such as Vail and Aspen. Millions of visitors also enjoy Colorado's many scenic wonders, such as Rocky Mountain National Park and Mesa Verde National Park, and do such activities as hunting, fishing, or attending rodeos, fairs, and other special events.

History

Native Americans:

A people known as the Basket Makers settled in Colorado's arid mesa country before the beginning of the Christian era. Later came the cliff dwellers, whose pueblos built into the canyon walls can still be seen today. The first Colorado settlers encountered Comanche, Cheyenne, Arapaho, and Kowa on the Great Plains, and Utes living in the mountains. These plains tribes united to fight the settlers, but were defeated in the Indian Wars (1861–1869) and the Buffalo War (1873–1874). Today, most Native Americans live on the Southern Ute reservation and in the Denver area.

Exploration and Settlement:

It is believed that the sixteenth-century Spanish conquistador Francisco Vasquez de Coronado was the first European to enter what is now Colorado.

Spain and France each claimed the territory for themselves during much of the eighteenth century, with France finally gaining the whole area in 1800. In 1803, the United States acquired the area from France as part of the Lousiana Purchase.

Territory:

Colorado became a legal territory on February 28, 1861.

Statehood:

Colorado became the 38th state on August 1, 1876.

Check It Out

For more information about the places in this book, check out the following web sites.

Colorado

Web site: http://www.state.co.us/

Cave of the Winds

Web sites: http://www.caveofthewinds.com/cave2000/
newsplash/splashtest.htm
http://www.goodearthgraphics.com/virtcave.html

Royal Gorge

Web sites: http://www.royalgorgeroute.com/
http://royalgorgebridge.com

Cripple Creek

Web site: http://www.cripple-creek.co.us/

Pikes Peak

Web site: http://www.pikespeakcam.com/camtop10.html

University of Colorado

Web site: http://www.colorado.edu/

Rocky Mountain National Park

Web sites: http://www.rocky.mountain.national-park.com/
http://www.coloradoguide.com/rmnp/frame1.htm

Also Available . . .

0-8010-4454-5 $5.99

Message in MONTANA

✖ When the Arlingtons find a used game at a local store in Message in Montana, they also find themselves on the first step in an exciting new quest. The family follows the cryptic clues from city to city, learning about the Lewis and Clark expedition along the way. What they find will take readers by surprise.

SOUTH DAKOTA Treaty Search

✖ In South Dakota Treaty Search, Ashley discovers a worn piece of paper in her new book, leading the Arlingtons to uncover the untold story behind the curious fragment. When they learn about an undisclosed government treaty, the family sets out to explore the Black Hills in search of the missing pieces of history.

0-8010-4451-0 $5.99

0-8010-4452-9 $5.99

Adventure in WYOMING

✖ When a family friend mysteriously disappears just hours after having served as their climbing guide, the Arlingtons set out to help in any way they can. Their sleuthing leads to more adventure than they bargained for, though, as they trek across the state on a clue-gathering mission that leads them to beautiful Yellowstone National Park.

Sports writer and newspaper editor **Bob Schaller** has won several awards for his journalistic excellence. Now a full-time writer, he is the author of The Olympic Dream and Spirit series, which covers athletes such as Mary Lou Retton, Dan O'Brien, Andre Agassi, and Dominique Moceanu. Schaller is also writing a biography of U.S. Olympic swimmer Amy Van Dyken. He lives in Colorado Springs, Colorado.